TAKE ME THERE

A Dare With Me Novel

J.H. CROIX

"Everything that's worth having is some trouble..."
~L.M. Montgomery

Sign up for my newsletter for information on new releases & get a FREE copy of one of my books!

http://jhcroixauthor.com/subscribe/

Follow me!
jhcroix@jhcroix.com
https://amazon.com/author/jhcroix
https://www.bookbub.com/authors/j-h-croix
https://www.facebook.com/jhcroix
https://www.instagram.com/jhcroix/

Chapter One

SKYLAR

I dashed across the parking lot to the public restroom. Too many seconds later, my bladder felt as if it let out a giant sigh when I made it into the stall and slammed the door shut.

"Finally," I muttered to myself.

"You know you're in the men's bathroom," a voice said.

"What?" I yelped before slapping my hand over my mouth.

Oh, my freaking god.

Fu-uuuuck, I hissed silently to myself.

There was no stopping my body now, though. The sound was way too loud for my comfort.

"Do you mind?" I ground out.

"I was in here first," the voice returned.

I could've sworn I recognized the voice and prayed it wasn't who I thought it was.

"Fine. I'm sorry I came into the men's bathroom." I flushed the toilet so I didn't have to hear the guy next to me peeing.

Another moment passed before I heard the stall door opening beside me. I considered just waiting it out, but I didn't want to be a coward. I pulled my dignity on, along with my pants, and walked out only to discover it was exactly who I feared.

Tucker Harrison stood there calmly washing his hands at the sink. He glanced over with a sly glint in his blue eyes. "Hi, Skylar."

Oh. My. God. I was usually able to speak, but Tucker could render me speechless even without me accidentally encountering him in the men's bathroom. I didn't want to admit I had a crush on him, but my body defied me every time I saw him. With his sky-blue eyes, rumpled brown curls, and a seriously fit bod, I got hot just standing near him. Now, we were in the men's bathroom together.

"Hey," I squeaked.

I almost ran out, but that meant not

washing my hands, so I cleared my throat. "Excuse me."

He turned off the faucet, stepping out of the way as he dried his hands on a towel. "All yours." He nudged his chin toward the sink.

"Thanks," I mumbled. My cheeks were burning up. I carefully kept my gaze lowered as I quickly washed my hands. "Are you going to leave?" I finally asked when I glanced over to see him waiting by the door.

"I was just trying to keep any other men from coming in while you're here."

"Oh, god," I finally said, feeling even more flustered. "I was in a hurry."

"Yeah, that was obvious," he replied dryly.

"Do you have to make it a thing?" I muttered when I shook the water from my hands.

"I don't know what you mean by that."

I snatched a paper towel out of the dispenser, drying my hands as fast as humanly possible then tossing it in the wastebasket.

Tucker even held the door for me as I walked out. Two strange men I'd never seen in my entire life waited out there. But then, this *was* a public restroom. I let out a sigh when they looked curiously at Tucker and me. I suddenly realized what conclusions they might be drawing from the fact that we'd been in the public bathroom together. I didn't know it was possible for my face to get any hotter, but the temperature climbed. Chin held high, I kept on walking.

One of the men chuckled as they walked in. "Hope it was good."

"Oh, my fucking god," I muttered to myself.

Tucker laughed softly as the door swung shut behind them and fell into step beside me.

"Why are you walking with me?" I ground out.

"Because I'm walking in this direction."

Of course. "Sorry, I won't make that mistake again."

"Oh, I bet not," he mused.

I glared at him. "Can we just move past this?"

"We already have. We're out of the bathroom. Moment over."

"Do you know who those guys were?"

"One of them is a new pilot. I'm not sure which airline he flies for."

Airline, in this case, meant a number of small airlines that flew lightweight, small planes in Alaska. That meant I would probably get to know the guy. I worked for a local air transport coordination business here.

"Ugh. Could you please clear up that misunderstanding?"

"I think the less said, the better, don't you? The guy who cracked the joke wasn't the new pilot. You can assume he was a random tourist."

Tucker stuffed his hands in his pockets as he walked alongside me.

"This is the longest conversation we've ever had," I observed.

He slid his gaze to mine. "What do you mean?"

"Just that. You're not exactly chatty."

"Is that a problem?"

"No, no." I felt a little defensive for making that observation. "Where are you going?"

"I'm actually going all the way to your office," he replied.

"Huh, why?"

"Because I need to stop by and pick up something for Flynn. I guess a delivery was left there for him."

"Oh," I said brilliantly.

When we arrived at the square industrial building where I worked, Tucker opened the door for me just as someone was coming through. The man turned too fast and bumped into me, bouncing me directly into Tucker.

Tucker was hard all over. His palm landed on my hip as he steadied me. A blaze of heat radiated from his touch. The man muttered an apology and jumped back before hurrying away. I practically sprinted into the building after a rushed goodbye to Tucker and hurried down the hallway into the back.

"What's up, Skylar?" Ludie Hill asked.

Ludie and Dan owned Diamond Creek Transport, which basically functioned as a sort of port for the wide array of items that landed here to be routed out to the smaller communities off the road system in Alaska. They also managed a local communication hub for the various small planes that passed through here, sending along safety messages and more. The business didn't make much sense anywhere other than Alaska. It was the most interesting job I'd ever had, and I loved it.

"Nothing, I was almost late," I said, hoping my flustered state could be chalked up to that. It had nothing to do with encountering Tucker Harrison in the men's bathroom and then having an actual conversation with him. Well, sort of a conversation. *Nothing* to do with that.

"You're not late," she said easily.

I immediately plunked down at the desk, putting on my headset and clicking open my computer screen. I couldn't believe I'd finally spoken more than a few words to Tucker. He probably hadn't even known who I was before. Maybe he knew my name. If that.

Chapter Two

TUCKER

The following day

"Dan loaded everything this morning," Skylar Bridges' voice came through my headset, low and throaty.

I doubted she knew I looked forward to hearing her voice every single day. I was getting ready for takeoff and had called over to check on the status of the delivery I was scheduled to fly across Kachemak Bay. I flew small planes for Walker Adventures. I loved flying, and I loved my job. Best of all, the company was owned by one of my best friends from the Air Force, so everyone there was like family to me.

I smiled, thinking about how flustered Skylar had been when I'd accidentally encountered her in the men's room the other morning.

"Got it. I'm taking off in a few minutes."

I was flying two tourists along with some cargo across the bay. After I signed off, I hopped in the plane, did my pre-flight checks, and reflexively glanced into the mirror to make sure both passengers had their seat belts on. It was a couple traveling to Seldovia.

After taxiing toward the runway, I waited until another plane landed before I took off. While Diamond Creek, Alaska, had a regular airport for commercial planes, this airport was adjacent to that one with a shorter runway for the lightweight aircraft that filled Alaska's skies. So many communities were off the road system that flying was the only way to reach them and bring in supplies.

I pondered Skylar's comment yesterday about me not being chatty. I knew it was accurate. However, it'd surprised me. I was so used to hearing her voice it felt as if I had talked to her a lot more. But those were mostly one-way conversations. Skylar handled the radio calls for this little hub in Diamond Creek, Alaska. Rural though Diamond Creek was, the town had a busy little airport. Over fifty flights came in and out daily, all small planes with a mix of tourists, supply delivery, and residents from the smaller communities traveling in and out for various appointments and shopping. It was a unique situation anywhere outside of Alaska. As a pilot from my military days, this allowed me to fly in a fun way.

Although I knew Skylar's voice well, I didn't see her often. She was hard to forget, though. She had brown hair and wide blue eyes. She kept to herself as far as I could tell. Seeing as I did as well, I understood. Alaska was a good place for that. She'd shown up in town just last summer.

Savoring my privacy, I preferred to keep my social world small. Even though I could admit I noticed Skylar in a *major* way, I needed to keep a clear boundary with her. Not because of her, but me. All I ever wanted was casual, and Skylar tugged me to her in a way that tested my discipline. My last serious relationship ended in a cold, sterile hospital. I preferred not to repeat that experience.

I kicked her out of my thoughts. I didn't need to dwell on Skylar, not today, not ever.

Many hours later that evening, I rolled my preferred plane into one of the hangars for Walker Adventures. I ran through the usual checks on the plane at the end of the day before locking the hangar and walking toward the parking area.

I stopped to look up at the sky, my breath catching in my throat. Alaska could do that to anyone. Tonight, the sunset was outdoing itself. The sky was painted with streaks of tangerine and red, fading into gold along the edges. The stars were breaking through the colors, and the moon was rising low above the mountains. On the heels of a breath, I began walking again and touched my keys in my pocket.

My boots crunched on the gravel as I angled across the parking lot toward my truck. I came to an abrupt stop when I heard what I thought was the sound of a sob. Glancing around, I didn't see anyone at first. Then I heard the muffled noise again. The only reason I knew someone was there was I saw the last rays of the sun catching on the top of someone's head, someone with dark hair.

I didn't even know what vehicle Skylar drove, but I suspected that was her. I told myself it was none of my business, and maybe she wasn't crying. Of course not. She couldn't be crying. But my feet veered in her direction when I began walking again.

"Everything okay?" I called, striving to keep my tone nonchalant.

Her head whipped up as she spun around. "Fine. Everything's fine." Her voice was clipped with a sharp edge.

Clearly, everything was not fucking fine. I could see the tears smeared across her cheeks. My heart twisted a little. "You sure?"

"Uh-huh." Her hand was resting on the top of a small hatchback.

"That your car?" I asked, curiosity getting ahead of my brain telling me to shut the fuck up and stop asking any questions.

She nodded. "Yep." There was a cargo compartment on top of it. It looked a little worse for the wear.

"Going somewhere?" I asked, gesturing toward it.

Looking a little sheepish, she shook her head. "No. I guess I could take it off."

I shrugged. "Not if you need it."

I stopped at the back of her car. I felt as if I were watching her pull on her composure like a jacket.

"It's sentimental, really," she offered.

"What do you mean?"

"I was supposed to come to Alaska with

my best friend. That was hers. She got it for the trip but never made it."

"Ah, so she decided not to come?"

I didn't know how to describe the expression that passed across Skylar's face, but it was a mix of emotions—sadness, anger, and deep hurt mingled with a dash of bitterness. She nodded. "Yeah, that's one way to put it."

"Well, you might want to fix the latch on the other side," I commented.

"What?" She scurried around the back of her car, eyeing it from below. "What do you mean? You're taller than me, so I can't tell."

"It's this," I reached up and tapped the inside of the latch on the racks supporting the cargo container. One of the bolts was coming loose. "You want me to take care of it?"

"I can't reach it very well," she said.

Stepping closer to stand beside her, I reached up and wiggled the lock. "Do you have a key?"

"Here." She reached into her pocket and handed me her keys.

Our fingers brushed, and it felt as if lightning sizzled up my arm. I turned the key in the lock before reaching around to adjust the casing and manually tightening the bolt. "There. You might want to get a wrench to tighten it more fully, but it should hold. I used to have these same racks on my old car. They loosen up after a while if you leave them on. Just check it occasionally if you're going to keep it up there."

"I should probably just take it off." She let out a quick breath.

"Not my call. Anyway, have a good night," I said. The lightning that had sizzled up my arm felt like it was spinning fire into every cell, sending a jolt of electricity to my entire system. I backed away, lifting a hand. "Catch you later."

"Thanks." Her throaty voice carried through the quiet sounds of dusk as I crossed the parking lot.

I waited until she climbed into her car and left. The sound of magpies chattering reached me, and I smiled to myself. This time was for owls, but magpies were bossy. They pushed into the space of every bird. I climbed into my truck and drove home. The drive was twenty minutes or so, and beautiful every mile along the way.

Chapter Three

TUCKER

It was almost fully dark by the time I came to a stop in front of Walker Adventures. Pocketing my keys, I smiled to myself as I crossed the parking area to the steps of the lodge. I had a sweet job, including a fabulous place to live. The main lodge was an octagon-shaped building. The lights were blazing tonight.

Flynn, one of my best friends and the guy who called me up after our years in the Air Force and offered me a job, had worked himself to the bone getting this place going. The lodge was fully self-sufficient with solar and wind power. And, damn, with seven pilots and counting, we stayed busy.

Flynn was taking on a few part-timers in town to keep up with the business for flights.

We also housed guests at the lodge, up to thirty at any given point in time. Along with the guests came amazing fucking food every night. I didn't stay in the lodge anymore. We'd built housing for the full-time staff nearby, but I still got dinner. I'd have been crazy to turn that down.

When I crossed through the main room, the low hum of voices reached me. This main room had several areas for guests to hang out. There was a big fireplace, a reading area, couches, and even a TV. Guests usually sorted themselves and sometimes mingled. I made a beeline through that area into the kitchen. Some guests were already seated at the long table that ran the length of the windows. I aimed for the area at the counter that faced the kitchen area, where the staff usually sat.

"Hey, man," I said as I slipped my hips onto a stool beside Grant, Flynn's younger brother.

He cast me a quick grin. "Hey, how's it going?" Grant shared the same coloring as Flynn—dark blond hair and slate-blue eyes with a dark rim around the edges as if they'd been etched in charcoal.

"How were your flights today?" I asked.

"Good. Yours?"

"Same," I replied.

"Need a beer?" Grant asked.

"Always," Diego answered Grant as he came out of the pantry, holding a six-pack in hand.

"What are you doing here tonight?" I asked as he handed me a beer.

Diego was another of my closest friends. Flynn, Diego, Elias, Gabriel, and I had all been in the Air Force together. One by one, we'd made our way to Alaska after Flynn returned home here to take care of his younger siblings, all of whom were adults now.

"There was yoga class, and Gemma usually stays for dinner afterward," he explained, referring to his girlfriend and the new love of his life. "I'm not going to miss dinner. Did you go to yoga class?"

"No," Gemma said as she entered the kitchen. "He's a slacker, but so are you," she teased.

"Hey, I had flights," I countered.

"Same here," Diego replied. "I rode out here with Grant, so I need to ride home with you." Gemma stopped at his side, and he pressed a kiss on her cheek.

"Of course, I'll give you a ride home." She smiled up at him.

"If you want to complain about my schedule, you need to talk to Nora," he offered with a wink.

"I'm teasing. Nora wasn't even in class tonight."

"You know how busy we are. It's only spring, and it's already crazy right now," Diego said. "Do you want a beer?"

"I'll drive home, so no thanks," Gemma said.

Diego sat down on my other side, and I lifted my beer to take a swallow. "What's for dinner?" I called over to Daphne, who was moving at the speed of light at the stove.

She glanced over her shoulder, replying, "Stir-fry with seared chicken and a maple glaze."

"Oh, wow. That sounds good. Have you made that before?" I asked after another sip of beer.

"Cat found the recipe," Daphne replied with a smile.

At eighteen, Cat was Grant, Flynn, and Nora's youngest sister and officially employed in the kitchen with Daphne. Flynn had landed in the lucky zone with Daphne. When she'd come out for vacation two summers ago, Flynn had fallen in love with her, and she was a to die for chef. We scooped her right up, or rather he did, and now she was here all the time. We all loved her.

"Good work, Cat. I'm sure it'll be fucking amazing," I called over.

Flynn had just entered the kitchen from the door to the back hallway. "Seriously, man. I'm trying to lay off the swearing."

"Why? You swear, Cat swears," I offered with a grin.

Cat laughed and rolled her eyes.

"I know, but if we ever have kids, I need to get better about it," Flynn explained with a sheepish smile.

Daphne looked at me and shrugged. "I did not ask him not to swear. You can swear all you want. I swear."

"It's good to be here tonight," I said after taking a long pull from my beer.

"It's always good to be here," Diego replied. "How are things at the house?"

"I sleep there, and that's it," I replied dryly.

He chuckled. "I know. How's Harley?" he asked, referring to his younger sister who'd moved out here last year.

"She's good. She's designing a new website for us," Daphne called over. "Ours is basic. She knows how to do the bells and whistles for us."

Diego flashed a quick grin in Daphne's direction, although she had already turned away. She buzzed around like a bee when she was in the kitchen.

"Harley's good at that stuff," he commented to me with Daphne otherwise occupied.

"I'm psyched she's doing that, but we're busy as it is. What the hell will we do with more business?" Grant mused.

"I barely have enough time to breathe from spring to fall, and even winter's been staying busier," I added. "I don't mind, though. I love being in the air."

"Don't we all?" Nora chimed in as she approached the counter. "I might need to rearrange the schedule next week."

"How come?" Diego asked.

"Does it matter?" she returned pointedly.

Diego shrugged easily. "Not really. I just like to know what I'm doing, so my schedule syncs with Gemma's."

Nora smiled warmly. "I'm so happy you're in love."

"And we are all so happy you and Gabriel are too," I teased.

Nora eyed me. "What does that mean?"

"You two were cranky when you were

trying to hide what was going on. That's all," I replied.

Her cheeks flushed pink just as Gabriel happened to appear, hearing only the tail end of my comment. "We're not hiding anything." As if to prove his point, he stopped behind Nora, slid his arms around her waist, and rested his chin on her shoulder.

They had to earn their second chance, or rather, Gabriel had because he was a dumbass.

"What about you?" Gabriel asked, glancing in my direction.

"What about me?" I countered.

"Are you seeing anyone?" Diego asked.

"What? Are we gossiping about me now?" I returned.

"No, we're just curious," Nora said.

"Nosy is more like it," Harley offered as she came in from the back door, casting her brother a look.

"Oh, don't even get started. You are the worst about being nosy," Diego said flatly.

"What do I have to be nosy about now?" Harley replied, her brows hitching up.

"You're nosy about me," her brother returned.

Harley shrugged. "When are you and Gemma getting married?"

I started laughing, relieved they weren't going to dwell on me. Romance wasn't my thing. I'd fallen in love once in high school, and that had been enough. My girlfriend died, and I was over love. I never wanted to go through the hell of loss again.

Gemma rested her elbows on the counter between Diego and me, her honey-brown curls swinging around her shoulders. "I haven't seen you in yoga class in a few weeks," she commented, her eyes on me.

"What? I thought it was optional."

"It is, but it's for all of the staff, and it's important we be there." Daphne turned around, resting one hand on her hip as she pointed a spatula in my direction. "You need to relax more. You're always keeping to yourself."

"Oh, my god," I grumbled. "Fine. I'll come next week, but I need to finish flying sooner to make it on time." I really did enjoy the yoga class. "Take it up with Nora, though. She's the one who set up my schedule for the past few weeks."

"Nora!" Daphne exclaimed.

Nora smiled sheepishly. "I'm sorry. We've been so busy."

"We need to talk about hiring more pilots," Flynn said.

"Doesn't more pilots mean more planes?" Grant queried.

"Most definitely," Flynn said. "That's the challenge. I need to run the numbers and talk to the bank. Meanwhile, you can always call Trey. He likes to do at least one or two flights a week." He was referring to a friend and a local pilot who had sold his plane and business to Flynn last year because he and his wife had another baby, and he already had a full career as a lawyer.

"That's right," Nora said. "I'll text him right now and see if he can just be our regular late-flight guy on Wednesdays."

"I promise I'll be there next week as long as I'm not in the air," I said to Gemma.

She curled her arm around my shoulders and squeezed. "It's okay. We just like having everybody there."

"And I like being there."

"Plus, you don't have to talk," Harley offered.

I narrowed my eyes at her. "And what does that mean?"

"You're not the chattiest guy," she teased. "It's okay. I talk a lot. It's probably better that you don't talk as much as I do."

Conversation moved away from me and yoga, and dinner was delicious. Afterward, when the guests had filtered out, and it was just staff lounging at the dining room table, I glanced around. I was profoundly grateful to have this job. Flynn, Diego, Gabriel, Elias, and I had all been like family to each other in the Air Force. Elias wasn't here tonight, but he joined us every few weeks. He was happily married, to the surprise of all of us. I suppose, aside from me, he might have been the least likely to fall in love.

When Flynn took over his family's flight and resort business after his mother passed away, he reached out to us because he needed pilots. We all had jobs doing what we loved, living and working with each other. It was freaking awesome. I let my gaze travel to the view outside. The sun was gone, and the sky's violet background faded into darkness as the stars and the moon took over. When I heard Gemma say Skylar's name, I wasn't thinking when I glanced her way.

"Damn, that was fast," Diego said from my side.

"Huh?"

"She said Skylar, and you looked over really fast."

"So what?"

Diego simply chuckled.

"What about Skylar?" I asked, deciding

not to care that this might lead to questions from my nosy friends.

"I was just saying she's come to yoga class in town a few times, and I wanted to invite her out here. I don't think she has many friends," Gemma explained. "She's only been in town a few months, and she moved here all by herself."

"She did?" Now, I was downright curious, and I didn't even care.

"Yeah, it's kind of a sad story. She planned this trip with her best friend, and then her friend died, so she decided to take the trip by herself."

I thought about that moment a few hours ago when I thought Skylar had been crying. I was pretty sure she had, but she'd covered it up quickly.

"Damn, that's rough," Diego said.

"Life is rough sometimes," Daphne offered matter-of-factly. "You should invite her out on staff night. That's when we get to have friends out."

"It is? Is this a thing?" I teased.

Flynn's teeth flashed with his smile. "Daphne likes a schedule. Of course, you can invite friends."

"Like you've ever invited anybody," I retorted, wishing I didn't feel so defensive.

Later that night, I left the main lodge and returned to the staff house. At this point, Grant, Harley, and I were the only ones who stayed here. My thoughts kept boomeranging back to Skylar. My friends were incredibly important to me. I considered them family. I knew what it was like to lose someone who mattered and imagined it was hard for her to come to Alaska alone. That should have been my first warning about the state of my own heart when it came to Skylar.

Chapter Four

SKYLAR

Arms akimbo, I stared up at the empty cargo container on top of my car. I idly kicked the toe of my boot against a tire. This was the car Emily and I had bought together and shared for several years. I still had the registration from California with both of our names on it. It didn't matter that it was expired, and I had Alaska plates now. That battered slip of paper represented a piece of our friendship.

Because of the life I'd had, I couldn't help but wonder if someday somebody would show up and tell me I wasn't allowed to have the car. Growing up and bouncing around the foster care system, I was accustomed to everything getting taken away. Nothing was ever really yours. The one thing in life that had been a stabilizing force and steady through it all was my friendship with Emily. But she was gone.

That was why I drove around with an empty cargo container on top of the car. We had planned to fill it for our trip. Instead, I drove here alone. It had been empty for months. I ignored the tears stinging at the backs of my eyes and gulped in a breath of air. I opened one of the back passenger doors, standing on the inside edge to undo the latches. A short while later, I carefully hefted the lightweight compartment off the car racks all by myself.

I laughed as I set it gently on the ground. "There you are." I smiled down at it.

That was how bad it was. I talked to inanimate objects. I wasn't great at making friends. I wasn't great at making connections, period. That had been Emily's role in our life. Grief washed through me, and I took a breath to steady myself. I'd gone on this trip thinking I could somehow muster up some of her energy, that carefree quality where she had the boldness to walk up and say hi to strangers and somehow end up being friends with them. That really wasn't me, not me at all.

I contemplated what to do with this cargo container. Small problem: I tended to charge ahead without thinking about the next steps. I glanced back when I heard my name to see Tucker approaching. I silently sighed. He would probably think I was an idiot. I was going to ask him to help me put this right back on top of my car because I had nowhere to store it.

"How's it going?" he asked when he stopped beside me. He looked down at the empty cargo container with me. "What are you doing with that?"

"That's a good question," I said, casting him a rueful smile.

"What do you mean?" His lips twitched at the corners.

I felt tingly all over. Tucker didn't smile too often.

"You helped me tighten up the latches last week, but it's empty. I really don't need to carry it around, so I took it off. I don't know where to put it, though, and I can't take it home with me because I don't have any storage there. My apartment is small."

Tucker looked at me, and a slow smile stretched across his face. My belly swooped.

"That is a problem. You can probably leave it in one of our hangars," he offered.

"Really? Is that okay?"

"There's plenty of storage. I'll let Flynn and Nora know."

"Are you sure?" I asked doubtfully.

"I'm positive. They won't care."

He reached down and lifted the container easily, somehow managing to put the whole thing on one shoulder with his hand propped up on the outer edge.

"You're carrying that by yourself?" I squeaked.

He was already walking ahead of me. "Yep, that's the plan, Sky," he called over his shoulder.

I came to a dead stop, my heart stuttering and a wave of emotion hitting me so hard and fast I was grateful Tucker wasn't looking at me. Only one other person ever called me Sky—Emily. I gave my head a shake and swallowed, shoving my emotions down inside as I hurried to catch up with him.

"Are you really sure?" I asked again as he stopped and punched in a code on the keypad by the plane hangar door.

"I'm positive. Really. You can ask them yourself. Also, if you haven't seen Daphne lately, she wants to invite you out to the lodge for dinner."

"Daphne?" I repeated numbly because I couldn't absorb much of what he was saying.

"Yeah, you know, Flynn's fiancée?"

"Oh. Really?"

Tucker was already walking through the now open bay door into the hangar as he replied, "Really."

His voice echoed in the cavernous space. He walked over to one side and lowered the empty cargo container to the ground. It looked tiny in this space. When he turned back to me, he swung his arm in an arc. "See, there's plenty of room." He paused, a slight smile curving his lips. "Actually, you know what? I don't want you to say anything to Flynn or anybody about this."

"Um, why?"

That worried me. I didn't want to keep a secret.

"Because I want to see how long it takes them to notice. I bet they won't."

I felt my eyes go wide as I stared at him. "Seriously?"

"Yeah. You wanna bet?"

"No, I do not want to bet," I said firmly. "I'm already feeling a little weird about this."

"Relax, Skylar. It's not a big deal, I promise."

"But—"

"We're not going to argue about it. Come on."

He turned and started walking out. His footsteps echoed in the space. Once again, I had to hurry to catch up to him. I was on the short side, another joke between Emily and me. She'd been tall and willowy to my short and not-so-willowy. In another moment, we were back outside the plane hangar.

Tucker tapped a button, and the garage bay door closed. "So you won't say anything, right?" he prompted.

"I feel weird about it, but okay. You promise I won't get in trouble?"

Tucker made the sign of the cross in front of his chest. "If anyone cares about the cargo container, which isn't going to happen, I will take all the blame."

But it's—"

"It's just for fun, Skylar."

"Okay." I took a breath and let it out slowly as I nodded.

"Now, you'll get better gas mileage."

"What do you mean?"

"Those aren't the most aerodynamic, even the ones that are designed to be somewhat aerodynamic."

"Oh, I never thought about that."

I just stood there after that, not sure what to say next.

"So, will you come out to the lodge?" he asked.

"Huh?"

"For dinner. Daphne would love that."

"Um, when?"

"Tomorrow is usually our staff night."

I hesitated. I wanted to go because I really wanted friends. But I had a teeny tiny bit of social anxiety. It's possible that anxiety ruins my life sometimes.

Tucker cocked his head to the side. "Come on, say yes. If you say no, then Daphne will get on my case, and you'll probably hear about it from her. Gemma too. Daphne asked me to invite you if I happened to see you. She asked all of us to, so don't be surprised if someone else mentions it."

I snorted a laugh. "Okay, okay, I'll be there. How do I get there?"

He slipped his phone out of his jeans pocket. "What's your number? I'll text you the directions."

I quickly recited my number, and he entered it into his phone. A second later, I felt my own phone vibrate in my pocket and slipped it out to see that he had texted, *It's Tucker.*

"You can just give me the address," I said, glancing up.

"It's not that straightforward. There *is* an address, but it's off the beaten path. I gotta run. I have a flight."

"Oh, okay."

"See you tomorrow," he called as he jogged off toward a different hangar.

I realized I'd been standing there too long when he stopped and turned around, calling, "I hope someone is monitoring the transport channel."

I laughed. "I'm at lunch!"

Shaking my head, I hopped in my car and aimed it toward Misty Mountain Café. The parking lot was full when I pulled in. Pocketing my keys, I jogged inside and stopped at the back of the line. Although this place was always hopping, the line moved quickly. Cammi, the owner, also owned Red Truck Coffee, a beloved coffee truck near the harbor.

When I got to the front of the line, she smiled warmly at me. Cammi was pregnant with twins, which I only knew because there was a countdown written in chalk on the corner of the menu board. Well, that, and she looked very pregnant. Cammi was one of those people who was easy to be around. I grinned back, offering, "I never know if I'm going to see you here or at Red Truck."

She shrugged. "Well, it's guaranteed to be one or the other. What will it be for you today?"

"I'll take a chai tea, and..." I looked up at the chalkboard menu. "How about the turkey sandwich with pesto and goat cheese? I haven't had that one yet."

"I love that about you," Cammi said as she rang me up.

"What?"

"Some people find their favorite, and that's all they ever get. I don't think you've ever gotten the same thing twice when you come in."

I shrugged. "Probably not. I like to try new things. You have specials all the time, so the menu never really runs out."

She grinned. "It's people like you who keep me on my toes. If the menu starts getting stale, just let me know."

"Cammi, the menu won't get stale. Everything you make is amazing," I insisted because it was true.

"Thank you." She passed my change over the counter with my coffee.

I dropped the change in the tip jar and slipped over to the end of the counter to wait for my sandwich. While she was prepping the next order of coffees, she commented, "You're staying above Midnight Sun Arts Gallery, right?"

I finished a swallow of my coffee as I nodded. "I love it there."

"Well, then you know Risa."

"Of course. She's my landlady. She's really nice," I added.

"She's so nice you could probably get away with not paying rent," Cammi teased.

"I wouldn't do that."

Cammi quickly passed over two coffee drinks to the next set of customers, pausing to ring them up. When she returned to the espresso machine to make the next round, she added, "Sometimes Risa, me, and some other women get together in the evening. Maybe you could come."

I didn't even know what to do with this. Twice in a single day, other human beings invited me to do things socially with them. I stood there and blinked for a long minute before Cammi prompted, "Skylar?"

"Sure, I'd love that," I said slowly, almost having to sound the words out in my mouth.

Emily flashed in my thoughts—my one and only close friend. If I was ever going to have another friend, even just one, I would have to actually try to get over myself.

"Great. What's your number?" she asked.

For the second time today, I recited my phone number to someone who texted me in return to confirm. I replied with a smiley face. I felt a little braver with Cammi than Tucker. She didn't send butterflies tickling through my belly and make my pulse race. She was just a really nice, sweet person and easy to be around.

My only encounters with her had been here or at Red Truck Coffee, which she'd only recently re-opened for the spring, but I came to one or the other almost every day.

"I'll text you the next time we schedule one, maybe sometime next week," she said, all normal and oblivious to what a huge deal this was for me.

"Oh, okay. That'd be awesome."

"Sweet."

Someone called out my order just then, and Cammi snagged it from the window into the kitchen and passed it over.

"Thank you!" I called as she moved on to wait on the next customers in line.

I was smiling to myself as I walked out to my car. I'd promised myself I'd try to make another friend, maybe even more than one.

The world was kind of lonely on your own. I'd taken this trip, telling myself I was doing it for Emily. I'd hoped it would give me the fresh start I craved.

I didn't have roots anywhere. The only thing I could count on from my days in foster care was I stayed in the same town, just like Emily. That was how we stayed connected for all those years.

Chapter Five

SKYLAR

Don't miss the turn. There's no sign.

I laughed softly at the last two lines in Tucker's text with the directions to the lodge. It was a practical, entirely straightforward text—just a list.

My belly shimmied a little. "You're being stupid," I said to myself as I lifted my head and set my phone down on the coffee table.

I curled my knees up and wrapped my arms around them, resting my chin on my forearms as I stared out the window. Although my apartment was tiny, I didn't need more space. I also preferred cozy places. I felt like I could manage them.

The view was, simply put, spectacular. Midnight Sun Arts Gallery was in a row of shops on a boardwalk along the beach near Otter Cove Harbor. It offered a view of the boats in the harbor where I could watch as they came in and out, morning and evening. Beyond that, Kachemak Bay shimmered under the sunrise. This morning's colors were washed out—soft pastels brushed across the sky, pink and gold with just a hint of lavender. Mount Augustine was in the distance in the inlet, standing tall and alone.

I couldn't explain it, but the volcano itself felt alive, even from this far away. I felt as if it knew secrets the rest of the world didn't. A few clouds encircled its peak, one of them shot through with pink.

I took a breath and uncurled my knees, standing and walking across my living room into the bathroom. My apartment consisted of a living room and efficiency kitchen, a small bedroom, and a single bathroom. The kitchen was to one side with the counter facing directly out the windows over the view. When I washed dishes, I could enjoy the view. The only dividing line was where the hardwood floor shifted to tile in the kitchen area. It was a pretty blue tile, creating a splash of color in the space. Off to the side of the living room was a bathroom with the bedroom immediately beside it.

Emily had found this apartment online. We were supposed to stay here together. She was the planner. My heart pinched as I glanced over my shoulder once more to catch another glimpse of the morning sky. She would have loved it. She'd wanted to travel the world. She told me the one good thing she got out of years in foster care was accepting that she might never feel settled. Alaska had been on her bucket list.

She'd wanted to become a pilot to get over her fear of flying. She'd said it would be like exposure therapy. After the awful thing that had happened where we'd both been sexually assaulted by one of our foster brothers in a foster home, we went to therapy, and both went through exposure therapy to address our trauma. Of course, we'd gotten kicked out of the foster home, not him. It was his parents' home. The only comfort was the family lost their foster care license. Emily thought she'd create her own exposure therapy to treat her fear of flying. Instead, her fear had been borne out completely when she died from complications in the hospital after a plane crash.

Now, I was trying to fulfill her dreams and get through to the other side of the grief that swamped me sometimes.

I showered and got ready for work, rolling my eyes at myself as I mulled over what to wear. Since I was going to leave work and go out to dinner, I wouldn't have time to come back home. Before I left, I checked on my pair of guinea pigs, Squiggly and Pigley. They had quite the setup with three cages and connecting tunnels. When I was home at night, I would let them out and giggle while they scampered about the small space.

While feeding them some lettuce, I offered, "I'll be a little late tonight, so I'll leave a light on."

I turned on the light in the kitchen. They probably didn't care, but it made me feel better. A short drive later, I parked at work and glanced around, cataloging the vehicles and noting that Tucker's truck was here. He was probably already up in the air.

I hurried across the parking area into the large corrugated steel building at one end. The door clanged shut behind me, and I hustled down the hallway.

"Hey!" I called out.

Ludie and Dan Hill ran this place. Ludie was a blunt-talking woman who seemed ageless, though I'd guess her to be past eighty. Dan was on the gruff side, but his love for

Ludie shone so brightly, it was obvious he was a secret softie.

She looked up from her desk. "Morning. Dan has a headache. If you could relieve him right off, that would be awesome," she called.

Dan had the occasional headache, but he was always working no matter what. "Morning, Skylar," he offered with a nod.

I shrugged out of my jacket and dropped my purse on the corner of the desk, moving swiftly. "Good morning." I slipped into the chair at the other end of the L-shaped desk, immediately putting my headset on and adjusting to the volume I preferred. Monitoring the coordination and communication for transport for the small planes in this part of Alaska was an interesting job. I loved it. It was busier than you might think.

Diamond Creek was a hub town for smaller villages. As many as fifty flights came and went here daily, with many carrying cargo to smaller communities.

"I got it, Dan," I said, glancing over.

He slipped his headset off and cast me a wan smile. "Thank you." Dan was also a plane mechanic and stayed busy helping a number of the businesses here. There were officially six small airlines, along with charter companies. Those were a little different. They solely handled official chartered flights for tourists. Walker Adventures, where Tucker worked, did charter flights, but they also handled cargo and mail and flights among villages on the other side of Kachemak Bay.

I swung into my day, monitoring communication about transport, reporting about weather changes, and on occasion, chatting with pilots when there were breaks in the action.

I was finishing up when Ludie came in to take over for the last hour. She rested her hips against the desk and eyed me. "So I hear you're having dinner out at Walker Adventures."

My cheeks got hot as I spun around in my chair. "Yeah, Daphne invited me." That wasn't specifically true.

"I thought Tucker invited you," she said immediately.

My cheeks got even hotter, and I felt flustered. "He, uh, passed along the message from Daphne." That *was* true.

Ludie's eyes took on a sly gleam, crinkling at the corners with her half-smile. "I suppose so. That man likes you."

"What? Ludie!" I finally sputtered.

She grinned. "And you like him."

"I haven't even spent much time with him, Ludie."

She shrugged. "Whatever you say, darlin'. I like Tucker, though."

I tried to be all nonchalant and cool, something I'd never succeeded at, *ever*, in my entire life. "Um, he seems nice." Sheesh. *Nice* didn't even come close. Sure, he was nice, but he was also sexy in an easy, relaxed way that set my nerves alight and sent me spinning inside.

Blessedly, Ludie didn't dwell on Tucker. "It's a beautiful place."

"You've been out there?" I couldn't help but ask.

"Oh, sure. I knew Flynn, Nora, and Grant's mom. Nice lady. Her husband was an idiot and an ass. After she passed away, Flynn came back from the Air Force and took over. He brought that place up to snuff and then some. Anyway, don't miss the turn."

Noticing the time, I stood and slipped on my jacket. "I'll try not to," I replied.

"There's no sign," she called as I walked out.

I smiled to myself. "See you tomorrow, Ludie."

"That you will."

Chapter Six

SKYLAR

I stood outside the wooden double doors at Walker Adventures, wondering whether I should knock. The lodge was beautiful, situated on a rise looking out over a valley with a view of Kachemak Bay in the distance. There were still patches of snow from the winter melting in the field, but shoots of green were coming up, and the trees had started to fill out. I finally lifted my hand and knocked. A moment later, the door swung open, and Daphne stood there, wearing an apron.

"You didn't have to knock. We have guests in and out all the time," she said.

"I wasn't sure."

She smiled, sliding her hand through my elbow and guiding me inside. "Come on in."

I took in the space—windows everywhere, a tall ceiling, and what looked to be an open area for the guests. A couple watched something on the television in one corner, and a woman was reading in front of a wood-stove where flames leaped among the logs.

"I feel like I walked into a brochure," I murmured.

Daphne laughed softly, squeezing my elbow. "I know. It's weird for me because I live here."

"You do?"

"Uh-huh. Flynn, Cat, and I live in a private area in the back." She gestured vaguely in one direction as we crossed through an archway into a large kitchen. A long table was situated against a wall of windows, offering an almost panoramic view of the mountains and the bay. To the side was a gleaming kitchen. It was large and utilitarian, and a counter encircled it with stools for seating.

"Have you met Cat?" Daphne asked as she drew me over toward the kitchen area.

A young woman who I presumed had to be one of the Walker siblings—because she shared Flynn's coloring of dark blond hair and grayish-blue eyes—smiled over at me. Her hair was pulled up in a ponytail.

"I'm not sure if we've met," I replied.

Cat smiled. "I don't fly like everybody else. I've got years to work on my license," she offered. She wiped her hands on her apron, then held one out to shake mine.

Daphne released my arm, and I shook Cat's hand. "I'm Skylar. I work with Ludie and Dan."

"Oh, I bet that's a super-cool job," she said as she immediately returned to checking something on the stove.

"I like it," I replied. "It's kind of fun. So you want to be a pilot?"

"Eventually," Cat replied. "Daphne taught me how to cook, so that's what I do here."

Daphne had already started chopping vegetables. She gestured with her knife toward the counter. "Have a seat. We have hors d'oeuvres." Her eyes arced about the room. "Is anyone else here?"

"Don't worry, you know they'll be here soon," Cat said dryly.

As if on cue, Flynn came walking through a door toward the back. "Hey," he said, casting me a quick smile. "Thanks for coming out." He walked toward Daphne, pausing beside her and dusting a kiss on the side of her neck.

Her cheeks flushed pink as she smiled up at him and continued chopping.

"Do you want something to drink?" he asked as he stepped away and glanced at me.

"Water will do," I replied.

"We have beer, wine, and cider from the brewery," he added.

"I'll stick with water since I drove."

Flynn winked. "It's only twenty minutes, but half of it is gravel."

"I haven't been out of town except for Anchorage since I moved here."

"Haven't you been here a while?" Daphne asked.

"Yeah, since last summer." I shrugged. "I have driven up to Anchorage a few times for shopping."

"That's a weird thing about Alaska," Daphne offered. "It's nothing to drive more than four hours to get groceries. I'm from Georgia, right outside Atlanta. People would think you were crazy to drive that far for groceries there."

"I know," I agreed.

"Where are you from?"

"San Francisco."

"Oh, is that where you grew up?" Daphne prompted politely.

"Yep."

This was where I hoped the conversation would stop. I didn't have any family to speak of. Both of my parents had died. My father, in a fight in jail and my mother, from drugs. To this day, I wondered if I had siblings I didn't know about.

"Oh, is your family still there?" Daphne asked.

That was a natural question. I managed a polite smile. "No, both of my parents passed away." While true, it didn't capture the full picture.

"Oh, I'm sorry," Daphne said with a glance up at me. Her eyes were warm, and I thought she genuinely was sorry.

"Thanks."

I hoped that would be it, and it was. Daphne shifted to lighter topics. Thank goodness. She did give me a searching look, and I sensed she wondered about my life. I *was* sad about my parents passing. More than that, I was mostly sad for the waste of their lives. You didn't get to pick your parents, and not everybody should have kids. That was for sure.

Flynn disappeared into a nearby open doorway, coming out with bottles of beer and cider and offering me a glass of water. "You'd probably be safe if you had one drink. Dinner around here takes a few hours."

I smiled. "Good point. I'll try the cider. I haven't had it yet."

"You haven't?"

"No. I don't have much of a social life," I offered with a slight shrug.

"You can come out every Wednesday if you want," Daphne said. "It's staff night. Staff night means we can invite people out."

"Consider this a weekly invitation," Cat offered.

I smiled and nodded and didn't even know what to think of that. That was how socially inept and anxious I was.

A moment later, Nora appeared, coming through the same entrance I came through with Daphne. Then Grant came through the back door. Elias and Cammi arrived to a chorus of warm greetings. I couldn't help but wonder when Tucker was going to show up. I promptly reminded myself I shouldn't be wondering about that.

Diego arrived with Gemma, throwing me an easy grin when he saw me. "Hey, Skylar. You have my favorite voice."

"Excuse me?" I replied, puzzled by his comment.

"Over the airwaves. You're friendly. Some people really master being dry and flat," he replied bluntly.

I laughed. "Ah, Ludie definitely sounds pro when she's on the radio, and Dan's all business."

Diego nodded. "Right. And they both swear like crazy otherwise."

"Well, I don't swear that much," I said quickly. "That would get me in trouble." I didn't actually know if it would, but I loved my job and was glad to have it.

Diego shrugged. "Around here, probably not."

Gabriel appeared, coming through that same back door. I finally asked, "Where does that door go?"

Nora grinned. "It's the back hallway. Flynn and Daphne's apartment is off the hallway there, and there's another outer entrance. There's a path in the woods to the staff house and my house."

"It's not just your house," Gabriel chimed in.

She slid him a look. "I built it for me," she teased.

"Yeah, but I live there now," he protested.

Nora rolled her eyes. "Fine, it's our house."

"I also stay in the apartment," Cat added. "But I'm going to move out."

"Where are you going?" Flynn asked

quickly, glancing at her with his brows hitching up.

"I'm over eighteen now. I get to move to the staff house," Cat replied.

Flynn narrowed his eyes, but didn't say anything. Daphne pressed her lips together and slid her eyes sideways to Flynn. "He's struggling with this."

"Are you serious?" Flynn finally asked, his gaze pinned to Cat.

"You actually want me to stay in the apartment with you?" Cat countered.

Grant interjected, "I don't want you to move into the staff house with me."

Cat glared at him. "I'm going to have my own bedroom. It's just you, Harley, and Tucker now. I am eighteen, and I can do what I want."

Nora looked amongst her siblings and shrugged. "She can, you know," she offered matter-of-factly.

Flynn took a breath and let it out before taking a long drag from his beer. "Fine." His gaze swung to his younger brother. "You have to keep an eye on her."

Grant let out a put-upon sigh. "I'm not keeping an eye on her."

"Dude, I've been keeping an eye on all three of you for years," Flynn said wryly.

"I was a nightmare when Flynn came home," Nora said as she slipped her hips onto a stool beside me.

"Really?" I wasn't used to families arguing without it being a big deal. Despite the pointed comments, no one seemed upset beyond mild annoyance.

"Oh, yeah. I was sixteen and pissed at the world. Our mom had died, and it was hard," she explained.

"Oh, I'm sorry!"

"It's okay. I miss her still, but we get along fine now." She cast a warm smile at Flynn, though he wasn't paying attention.

"If you move out, we're turning that bedroom into something else," he said to Cat.

"My office," Daphne said quickly. "I need a space to do all the business stuff."

"There we go. It'll be your office. I'll set it up however you want," Flynn said.

"Wait!" Cat waved a spatula in the air, spinning in a circle. "Which bedroom do I get?"

"There are two empty ones. You can pick," Tucker said as he entered the kitchen and caught the tail end of the conversation.

"Awesome!" Cat beamed at him. "Will you guys help me move?"

"Sure," Diego, Elias, and Tucker replied in

unison while Grant and Flynn remained silent.

Daphne smiled amongst the group. "Well, that could've been much worse." Cat giggled as Daphne curled her arm around her shoulders.

Just having Tucker show up sent butterflies aflight and spinning in my belly. When his eyes landed on mine, his lips kicked into a smile. "You made it. You must not've missed the no sign spot."

"I followed your directions. Ludie said the same thing about the sign," I replied.

"We need a sign," Daphne announced.

Flynn glanced her way. "I'll put it on the list."

Nora was on one side of me, and there was an empty stool on the other. I told myself I did *not* care if Tucker sat there. He rounded the counter after picking up a bottle of beer, aiming in my direction. Seconds later, he was right there. Those butterflies went a little crazy, tickling my belly and sending tingles radiating in pulses through my body.

Chapter Seven

TUCKER

I rested an elbow on the counter and lifted my beer to take a swallow. Lowering it, I glanced toward Skylar as she responded to something Nora said. Skylar had a sweetness to her, and I didn't know what to make of it. It wasn't a quality that generally appealed to me.

Of course, I was also lying to myself whenever I tried to convince myself of that. Claire had been a sweet girl. She was the girl who rescued animals and tried to take care of everyone in her orbit. Then she got sick and fucking died before she even graduated from high school. It's not that I'd expected life to be fair. But that had made it crystal clear it absolutely was not.

Skylar's sweetness was different. There was a sharp edge to it. She covered it up with toughness.

"Yo, Tucker." Diego's voice reached me.

"What?" I asked.

He grinned. "Nothing, just trying to see how distracted you were."

I knew he'd spotted me noticing Skylar. He bit the inside of his cheek to keep from laughing. "I only said your name four times."

"You were busy staring," Elias added.

I rolled my eyes. "Whatever. How's life with Cammi?" I asked.

"It's always good," Elias replied.

"It's not always good. You were cranky yesterday," Cammi interjected.

Cammi was also sweet, a contrast to Elias, who could be a cranky ass. "He's always been cranky in the morning," I said. I caught his eyes again. "She's pregnant." I gestured to Cammi who was expecting twins. Elias was over the moon about it. "You should be nice all the time."

Cammi shrugged, but Elias rolled his eyes. "I hadn't had my coffee yet," he protested. "I swear, I'm not an ass to her."

Cammi chimed in. "You're not an ass, but you're driving me insane worrying."

Elias sighed. "I'm doing my best."

"Dude, you have your own personal barista," Diego said, gesturing toward Cammi, who laughed softly. "Just knowing that she's going to make you coffee in the morning should put you in a good mood."

To his credit, Elias looked a little sheepish. "Yeah, I know. I'm not that great in the morning."

"Yet you have a job where you have to get up early. Should I talk to Nora about your schedule?" Cammi teased.

"No," the four of us said in unison.

Elias grinned. "That's not an option. If I changed my schedule, I wouldn't see you much in the evenings. You're a morning girl, and I want as much time as I can get with you." My friend was deeply in love and didn't care to hide it.

"Aw, you're so sweet, Elias!" Cat called over.

I was grateful at the deflection of the topic from me as Diego continued to tease Elias, and they fell into their usual back and forth. When I glanced toward Skylar again, she was quiet, tracing her fingertip on the label of her cider bottle as she watched the interplay amongst everyone here.

"So, seriously, did you have any trouble finding it?" I asked.

She shook her head. "Even though you made sure to tell me there was no sign, you gave me some landmarks. It's a nice place. I think it's really cool you guys all live out here."

"Elias and Diego don't stay here anymore."

"Well, they obviously come out for dinner," she returned.

"They do. Gemma also teaches a yoga class here for staff once a week, and that's tonight," I explained.

"Oh, that's cool." Skylar glanced at Gemma.

Gemma's curls bounced as she smiled over at Skylar. "You can come to class in town, or here if you'd like."

"Oh, is it the same cost?"

"Actually, it'd be free here," Gemma replied. "Because the resort pays me."

"I feel like I need to pay."

"Well, then do two classes a week."

Skylar smiled again. "I just might do that."

I was curious about her, especially after what I had learned. I wanted to ask what happened to her friend. I wanted to ask what it was like to take this trip by herself. I'd driven up here by myself. It was a hell of a drive—beautiful, stark, stunning really, but long, and some stretches felt lonely.

Tonight wasn't the night for me to be curious, though, not with the audience of all of my friends. Daphne herded us over to the dinner table a little bit later. Skylar ended up seated across from me, and I promptly concluded that was a bad idea because I kept catching myself staring at her. She was right *there*.

She took a bite of the halibut glazed with lemon and maple, her eyes going wide before she moaned. "Oh, my god. Daphne, I've heard about your cooking, but wow."

Daphne smiled, brushing her auburn braid off her shoulder. "Thank you. I love to cook."

"Well, this is amazing. I know you make some stuff for Cammi, right?"

Cammi nodded. "Oh, yeah. Daphne gave me a head start at the café. We get a delivery every morning. I don't even know how you do it all."

"Cat helps," Daphne offered with a shrug. "We have a system, and we've got the guys for free delivery."

Skylar laughed at that, and dinner carried on. As the night wore on, I realized my draw to Skylar wasn't the smartest plan. I was cynical, not because anybody had ever broken my heart—unless I counted the cruelty of the universe. I didn't want to risk loving and losing. Not again. I'd argue the point on that quote about loving and losing being better than not loving at all. It hurt like hell to love and lose someone.

I could practically hear my sister chirping in my ear. She was a therapist, and she'd told me more than once she thought I was letting my grief hold me back. She didn't get it. There was a sad, sore point in my heart where Claire had once lived. But I was okay. The ache of missing her had faded to the point it felt like a ghost. She'd been gone long enough it was hard to imagine her being here. I just didn't want to be angry at the world all over again. Life was fickle, and shit happened. The longer I lived, the more deeply I understood that. Even when I had examples to tell me otherwise.

Daphne landed in Alaska after her son died of some rare cancer. It broke her heart. My mind, or rather my heart, didn't want to contemplate the fact that she had, in fact, found a fresh start here. She and Flynn were deeply in love, and she was clearly happy. My thoughts practically grumbled at each other as they rolled about like billiard balls in my mind. There was no strategy to whatever was directing them. They bounced against the edges and each other, ricocheting into points of pain.

I had a pretty good life with rock-solid friends I considered family and a job I loved. I didn't need to risk asking the universe for more.

"So, tell us about San Francisco," Daphne said at one point, directing her question to Skylar.

"Well, Alaska is definitely a change of pace," Skylar offered. Her gaze was careful.

"Do you miss San Francisco?" Cammi asked.

"I didn't have anything holding me down there." Skylar shrugged. "My best friend was supposed to come up here with me, but she died."

Her tone was almost flat, and I recognized the feeling behind it. That was how I talked about Claire. You practiced saying things. If you said hard things enough, they lost the punch of emotion right to the heart. It could start to feel hollow and caved in.

"Oh," Daphne said softly, trailing her fork through the leftover sauce on her plate. "I'm so sorry."

"It's okay." Skylar squared her shoulders a

little, her chin rising slightly. "Life happens, right?"

"Oh, that it does." Daphne's gaze was understanding as she looked at Skylar.

Skylar was looking down at her plate. I was distracted, and that annoyed the hell out of me. I didn't get distracted. That was why the Air Force had been such a good fit for me. I stayed focused and on point. Flying was perfect for my personality. Yet all it took was one woman to distract me at dinner with my friends. I knew I was going to hear about it later.

The group gradually filtered apart, and I found myself lingering when I would normally head back to the staff house. But Skylar was still here. She offered to help Cat clean up. When Daphne tried to dissuade her, Skylar shook her head. "You cooked. Let me help clean up."

"We've got it," Cat called, waving Daphne out of the kitchen.

Grant had his feet propped on an empty chair and was busy texting. I crossed over to the kitchen area, leaning my elbows on the counter.

Cat eyed me. "If you're gonna hang out, you need to work."

"What can I do?" I helped clean up sometimes, so this wasn't wildly out of the ordinary, but Cat gave me a suspicious look.

"Why don't you load the dishwasher?"

That put me beside Skylar. She was cleaning off plates and tossing napkins in the trash. She cast me a quick smile, but she was mostly all business. It didn't take long before we were done. I offered, "I'll walk you to your car."

Cat was conveniently in the bathroom, and Grant had wandered off. Skylar simply nodded and followed me through the front area, which was quiet now. Dinners on staff nights ran late mostly because we lounged around the table afterward. The lights were dimmed. I turned the outside lights on while Skylar shrugged into her jacket.

Once we reached the bottom of the stairs outside, she stopped and tilted her head back. The stars glittered in the darkness. "Wow," she breathed. "I don't think I've ever seen this many stars in my life." She glanced at me, her face shadowed. "You don't realize how much light pollution matters until there isn't any."

"I know."

Her breath misted in the chilly, late winter air. Technically, it was almost spring, but it didn't feel like it. Spring in Alaska wasn't warm.

"Thank you for inviting me," she said.

"Of course. I was just the messenger. It was Daphne's invitation."

"Please make sure to thank her for me. I don't think I had a chance before I left."

I suddenly felt like a jerk for pointing that out. "Maybe it was Daphne's invitation, but I wanted you to come too."

I surprised myself with that comment. Skylar had taken a step, and her boots crunched on the gravel as she turned quickly to face me.

"Oh."

"You have a standing invitation now, so make sure to come again."

Uncertainty chased through her eyes. "Really?"

"Of course. Trust me on that."

She searched my face, her doubts stamped in her eyes.

"Why do you seem so surprised?" I asked.

"Because." She shrugged. "I don't know why. I only had one close friend, and she died." I could feel the emotion behind her words, and the force of it took my breath away.

"I'm sorry about your friend. Life fucking sucks sometimes."

She looked up at me, her brows hitching slightly. "It does. Thank you for not trying to make that seem like anything other than what it was."

I nodded. She turned again, continuing to walk across the gravel parking lot. I followed. She stopped beside her car.

"Nobody's noticed your cargo container yet."

Skylar giggled. It was the first time I had heard her giggle, and the sound moved through me like sparks leaping from a fire.

"I can't believe no one's noticed."

"Promise you're going to keep that promise and not mention it," I teased.

She rolled her eyes. "I promise. I think it's ridiculous, though."

"It doesn't matter. Honestly, no one cares. They care so little they haven't even fucking noticed it."

Her shoulders shook when she giggled again. The sound petered out, and we were staring at each other in the moonlight. We were beyond the soft glow of the light cast from the entrance to the lodge. Skylar looked up at me as if she wanted to say something. Except I didn't really want to talk.

I took one step, and then I was standing right in front of her. Lifting my hand, I trailed my knuckles along her cheekbone. Her eyes were like pools of starlight under the moon. I sensed she was waiting to see what I would do, so I let my instincts take the reins. Even though I didn't do romance, I was an expert at casual. Maybe that was all I needed with Skylar. We could be friends with benefits.

I lowered my head, moving slowly enough she could dissuade me. She didn't. Her eyes held mine all the way until my lips brushed over hers. It felt as if a shock of electricity zapped from her to me. I didn't know who gasped. I angled my head and slid my hand into her hair.

As I fit my mouth over hers, her body went taut before she let out this little sigh, her breath hitching in the back of her throat. At the sound, it felt as if lightning sizzled through my body, the heat of it so intense I felt singed inside.

She pressed closer, and I felt the soft give of her curves. I suddenly felt greedy and slid my hand around her waist, down over the sweet curve of her bottom. As I pulled her close, I let my tongue tangle against hers. She startled me by kissing me boldly. She pressed closer again and just as quickly drew back on a gasp, jumping away as if I had shocked her.

She'd shocked me, and my heartbeat was thundering. Her hand pressed against her heart, our breath misting in the air as she stared at me.

"What was that?" she whispered.

"A kiss."

"Don't ruin this. Please."

Before I could ask what she meant, she was climbing in her car and slamming the door. I stepped back, watching as she drove away until her taillights disappeared down the long driveway a moment later.

"Ruin what?" I asked the ceiling in my bedroom a little while later.

Chapter Eight

SKYLAR

"Why did I say that?" I asked myself as I ran a brush ruthlessly through my hair the following morning. "Tucker's going to think I'm crazy. And now I'm talking to myself."

My reflection had nothing to say in return. Feeling foolish, I tugged off my T-shirt and leggings and climbed in the shower, hoping the steaming hot water would clear my head. It had been really nice to hang out with everybody last night. I thought maybe I could make friends. But if Tucker was going to go and kiss me, that would ruin everything.

I had serious deep-seated and intractable abandonment issues. I tended to get clingy *real* fast when it came to guys. The way I'd managed that little issue for the past few years was to never get involved with anyone. That was worse than trying to make friends. My entire childhood had been colored by a desperate craving to feel like I belonged somewhere, to have a family and someone who loved me.

When high school came along, I was like a little barnacle when it came to guys. I didn't do anything crazy, like stalk someone, but I was crushed at even typical breakups. I'd had several therapists during that stretch, and they'd all tried to help me understand my pattern and that it was okay to have those issues. They'd told me I would have to figure it out in order to have a healthy relationship. After the last breakup a few years ago, I decided it wasn't worth it to keep trying. I couldn't seem to persuade my heart to listen to my brain.

I resolved it was best not to try to have a relationship because I tumbled into feeling nervous, skittish, and anxious followed by being needy and clingy. Then to prevent the eventual rejection from coming, I would sabotage. I was black belt–level skilled at sabotaging relationships.

My life worked better when I didn't put myself in situations where I got emotionally needy. The one and only person who had always been there for me was Emily. And now, she was gone. As Tucker had so eloquently put it, *life fucking sucks sometimes.*

When I got to work that morning, I was relieved Ludie was ensconced in her office working on accounting stuff. Dan immediately logged off once I had my headset on. I could lose myself in coordinating cargo transport, providing weather updates, and more. I wondered if I would hear Tucker's voice at any point today.

The second I wondered that, my skin got all hot and prickly because our kiss might've been brief, but—sweet hell—it was so good. He even tasted good, a little minty. He smelled like the ocean with a hint of spruce underneath, which was kind of weird. But I suppose it was Alaska. He smelled like where he lived, and I loved that. I was going to be all up in my head and wished I had something, anything, to distract me.

When my phone vibrated with a text message, and I saw it was Cammi, I practically cheered.

Cammi: *Hey, I know it's short notice, but if you can, come by Misty Mountain Café after eight tonight. We're gonna have a late dinner and hang out. We'd love to see you.*

She added a flower and a heart, which was so Cammi. I didn't even let myself obsess about it. I replied right away because I needed a distraction.

Me: *I'd love to. I'll be there. Thanks for thinking of me.*

That got me another heart and another flower.

When I parked outside Misty Mountain Café, I tried to ignore the nervous feeling inside. My chest felt tight, and I was stiff all over. Socially, it was fair to say I didn't have the best skills. It was hard to learn them in foster care. Like most foster kids, I'd been too busy trying to read the room of every new home I was in and suss out what to do next. The safest option was to hold back because you never knew who you could trust.

The café was in an old Quonset hut, which was pretty common around here. The curved corrugated steel structure had been transformed into a whimsical place. There was a colorful sign, and the inside felt open and airy with artwork hanging on the walls and pretty painted tables. I tucked my wallet in my pocket and took a deep breath.

Squaring my shoulders, I climbed out of the car and approached the building.

This shouldn't have been a big deal. It was just dinner, and Cammi was nice. I couldn't imagine any of her friends being anything other than completely lovely. When I peered through the window, I saw Cammi at the counter talking to my landlady, Risa. I relaxed a little. Risa was also welcoming.

I wasn't sure if I should knock. As I contemplated this, another woman looked over, one I didn't recognize. She waved at me through the windows, and I pushed through the doorway, pausing when Cammi lifted her head. A smile broke across her face. "Hey, Skylar! Glad you could make it."

She rounded the counter, and Risa walked over with her. "Hey, you! How's the apartment?" Risa slipped her hand through my elbow and gave it a squeeze.

"It's perfect," I said honestly.

"I'm so glad you like it."

"Are you going to need to rent it when summer comes?" As soon as I asked that question, I mentally bopped myself upside the head. Now was not the time for this conversation, but my anxiety tended to bubble up like that.

"No, I don't do the tourist thing. It's a lot of work."

"Are you sure?"

Risa smiled again, squeezing my elbow once more. "Of course, I'm sure. It's your place as long as you want to stay there."

"She's already heard the rumors about the summer rental nightmare," Cammi said from Risa's other side.

"Oh, are there rumors about that?" Risa asked.

Cammi rolled her eyes. "Of course. Apartments are like gold come summer."

"I honestly don't want to deal with it. I'd have to clean the room every day, change the sheets, do all the touristy stuff," Risa explained. "I am happy to have a good tenant stay there all summer. I've even left it empty sometimes when I don't have it rented yet."

"Are you serious?" the woman who waved at me asked. Her dark curls bounced around her shoulders when she turned to look at me. "You must be Skylar."

I nodded. "This is Susie," Risa said from my side as she freed my elbow. "Don't be too nosy, Susie," Risa warned.

"Nosy? I'm not nosy," Susie protested.

"Bullshit," Daphne said.

Glancing over, I saw she was sitting at a table.

"Oh, hey," I said.

She lifted her hand in a wave. "Nice to see you. This is one of our girls' nights."

"Thanks for inviting me." My gaze found Cammi, and I smiled.

"You lucked out. Daphne doesn't get to come very often, and she brought leftovers from the lodge," Cammi said conspiratorially.

"Ooh, I get your food twice in a week. I feel blessed," I said.

"I keep telling Daphne she should open a restaurant in town. I know the lodge loves you and all that," Susie said as she sat down with a flounce beside Daphne. "But Diamond Creek could use a new restaurant, a little competition."

Daphne laughed softly. "I really like my setup right now. I've done a full-time restaurant, and it is a *lot* of work."

"Isn't what you do already a lot of work?" I asked, sitting down when Cammi gestured for me to take a seat beside her.

"Yeah, but I can manage it. I cook for the guests at the lodge, so it's a set number all the time. Then I do the extras for fun, like Cammi's sandwiches," she explained. "I had a restaurant before. And, well, that kind of thing can run you into the ground."

"Oh, where was that?" I asked.

"In my other life in Atlanta." Daphne waggled her eyebrows, smiling slightly. "I did enjoy it, and it was a good experience, but I don't need the rush."

"Diamond Creek is not Atlanta. I don't think it'd be as busy," Cammi pointed out.

Daphne eyed her skeptically. "Tourist season is insane here."

Susie found that hysterical and burst out laughing. The bell above the door chimed, and I glanced over to see two more women entering—Gemma and Nora.

"Oh, it's almost everybody who was at dinner last night except the guys," Nora said when she sat down beside me. "We need a break from the guys sometimes."

"What do you think about Diamond Creek so far?" Susie asked. "You work for Ludie and Dan, right?"

"I do. I love it."

Nora smiled over at me. "Skylar's perfect at manning those transports and reporting calls. She knows when she can be conversational, but she's all business. Ludie's always a little too loud for me ever since she started going deaf."

Susie laughed again. "That's why she talks so freakin' loud."

"I swear my ears hurt when she's on duty. They're going to need to retire soon. You should talk to them about taking over the business," Nora offered.

"What?!" I yelped.

Unfazed, Nora shrugged. "Why not? You're already trained."

"I, um, I don't know," I sputtered.

"If you decide to go for it, ask me for help," Susie said.

"Uh, okay?" I returned, uncertain of what she meant.

Cammi smiled. "Susie's an accountant. She's also really good at helping you figure out the loans with the bank. She helped me buy this place."

My mouth dropped open as I looked from Cammi to Susie. Cammi slipped her arm over my shoulders and gave me a light squeeze. "It's just a thought."

The mere idea of running my own business seemed so impossible I didn't even know what to think. I didn't know how to explain how crazy that idea was for me. I felt ridiculous for feeling like it was so ridiculous and even more ridiculous for the whole thing. I'd never had much of anything to call my own.

"I haven't even heard Ludie and Dan talking about retiring," I finally said.

Susie shrugged nonchalantly. "She's not young. I'll ask my mom. She'll know."

"Your mom?"

"Yeah, she's friends with Ludie. Ludie's even older than her."

"Your mom isn't that old," Nora offered dryly.

"She's sixty-four," Susie replied. "And Ludie's like eighty or something."

"She's that old?" I prompted.

Nora nodded. "Oh, for sure."

Anxiety tightened in my chest. Worry was a constant when you never had any stability in your childhood. Any threat of change warranted hours and hours upon hours and hours of concern. Emily had been less of a worrier than me but not by much, really.

Susie leaned an elbow on the table, casting a smile at me. "I'm your girl. We're going to find out the scoop and come up with a plan."

I nodded, and a timer sounded. Cammi jumped up. "Be right back. That's dinner."

Daphne got up to help, and a few minutes later, they returned with several casserole pans filled with tamales.

Only moments later, I took my first bite.

"Oh, my god," I moaned. "These are so good."

"I love making them. I made a batch for lunch today, and I made extra because I knew we were meeting tonight. I had to hide them from Flynn."

"He doesn't even know?" Nora whisper-shouted across the table.

Daphne grinned as she shook her head. "If any of the guys knew, they'd all be gone. Cat had to go into town for some appointments and errands, and that's when I made them."

"Wow, I feel spoiled," I commented.

"Don't. You have a standing dinner invitation with us every week."

"And you can come here anytime we get together. I'm not as organized, though," Cammi said quickly.

"You all don't have to invite me to everything," I heard myself saying.

Daphne eyed me quizzically. "We want to," she finally said. "We like you, Skylar."

My throat got tight. I didn't know what to say, so I stuffed a bite of food in my mouth, relieved when the conversation moved along. I enjoyed listening to the chatter about people I didn't even know and watching the light-hearted teasing amongst everyone. I eventually put together that Cammi, Nora, and Susie had grown up here. Risa had grown up outside of Anchorage, but her brother lived here. She moved down here and was married to the police chief. I'd seen him, but I hadn't connected those dots yet.

"So I better not get caught speeding," I commented.

"Oh, just stay under nine miles an hour over the limit," Risa replied matter-of-factly.

"What do you mean?" Susie chimed in.

"The police don't usually pull anyone over unless they go more than nine miles an hour over the speed limit. Well, unless you're a repeat offender," Risa offered with a shrug.

"Wow, that's good to know. I wonder if that's the case everywhere," I replied.

Susie giggled. "That's what I'll set my cruise control on."

Daphne was new to the area, along with me. "How long have you been here?" I asked.

"About two years."

"She was supposed to only stay for a month," Nora offered with a grin. "But she fell for Flynn, and Flynn fell for her, and now they're getting married. We are all grateful. He's kind of a grump. That's his baseline. Daphne brings his mood up significantly."

"Getting regular sex helps, I'm sure," Susie offered dryly.

"Oh, god. Don't talk about my brother's sex life," Nora muttered.

Daphne laughed.

Just when I thought no one would ask any more questions about me, Nora looked at me, arching a brow. "So, Tucker?"

"Are you talking to me?" I hedged. She nodded slowly. Daphne pressed her lips together, and I could tell she was trying not to laugh. "What are you talking about?"

"You kissed him," Nora said bluntly.

My cheeks got fire hot. "What? How do you know?" I sputtered.

"It was in the parking lot. Gabriel and I went out the back and saw you on the way over to my place."

"Oh, my god." I leaned my face into my hands and took a deep breath. "Wow. I don't even know how that happened. I'm gossip. It was just a kiss," I finally said when I found the nerve to lift my head again.

"Tucker is a really great guy," Daphne offered.

"I don't know what I was thinking. I have no expectations, and I'm pretty sure he has no expectations from me. I won't be kissing him again," I said quickly.

"We want him to have expectations," Nora said, slapping her palm on the table.

"Do tell," Susie said. "I know Tucker, but I have no gossip about him, like none. That guy seriously flies under the radar around here, which is hard to do in Diamond Creek."

Since the kiss was already out there, I decided I didn't need to hold back and was unabashed in my curiosity. "What do you know?"

"Like everybody at the lodge, except for me, Daphne, Cat, and Grant, all the guys were together in the Air Force. They are tight, and Tucker is awesome. He doesn't date, though. To be honest, I don't even know if he gets any on the side. I asked Gabriel, and all he did was shrug, but those guys do keep secrets amongst themselves," Nora explained.

"I know they do," Daphne said. "Flynn usually tells me everything though."

"Yeah, because he's whipped," Cammi piped up.

Daphne rolled her eyes.

"What else do you know about him?" I asked.

"He has a younger sister. She's a therapist. Both of his parents are alive, and he's close with them. Flynn said something sad happened with his high school girlfriend, but I don't have the details. I'm going to ask Tucker myself," Daphne said, drumming her fingertips on the table.

"The guys tell Daphne everything," Nora commented. "They look at me as Flynn's little sister, so they don't do that with me."

"But Gabriel doesn't," Daphne teased.

Nora's cheeks flushed pink. "I tell you everything too, so get the scoop."

"I think you and Tucker would be good together," Cammi said. "I've always liked him. He's nice, but he's pretty quiet."

"Elias is quiet," Susie chimed in.

"Yeah, but he's also kind of broody. Tucker isn't like that," Cammi replied. "He's just plain quiet."

"You know, you all aren't helping me on the information front," I pointed out.

"Well, do you like him?" Susie asked.

My heart thumped in my chest, and my breath got short for a moment. "I don't know. I mean, yes, I guess," I finally said, feeling way too flustered. Having chats about crushes wasn't something I did, except with Emily. Who was dead. I took a shaky breath.

"We need a new romance around here," Susie said with a gleam in her eyes.

Chapter Nine

SKYLAR

Sitting on the couch, I wrapped my arms around my knees with my chin resting on them and stared out the window. The inky black surface of the ocean glittered under the moonlight.

I was pretty sure Susie was crazy to think Tucker and I could have anything like a romance. That kiss was a fluke. Plus, me and romance equaled total disaster. I knew what would happen. I'd start to panic because it was easier to stay abandoned than to let myself hope for something else.

I sighed. "What should I do, Emily?" I whispered into the darkness.

You could give yourself a chance.

Sometimes, I felt like she talked to me,

but then I felt a little crazy. She said that a lot—that we should give ourselves a chance. She would say it to herself and to me.

When I'd traveled to Alaska, in part, I'd done it because the trip was already set up. She'd found the rental for us. We'd applied for jobs together, and I'd been shocked when I'd gotten one after a video interview.

I came here thinking I would do what Emily said and give myself a chance. In all of that, romance was never in the equation. Simply finding a life and landing on my feet felt like a freaking miracle.

On the heels of another sigh, I unfolded my legs, wondering whether I should try to go to bed. Sleep didn't come easy to me. Ever. I'd also never lived alone before this. After foster care had bounced us out when we turned eighteen, Emily and I had lived together in whatever we could afford. Sometimes, it was in one-room apartments, but it was always us.

It was weird to be alone. Emily had liked to sleep with a television on. I was trying to break that habit, but it was hard.

It was quiet here in Alaska, quieter than anywhere I'd ever lived in my entire life. Once the gallery shut down, it was just me in the apartment upstairs. Down the hallway,

Risa rented out a room to an artist who I'd yet to meet. I'd heard her working in there a few times. She was never here at night, though. I padded into my bedroom, tugging the sheets and quilt over me and lying there. My mind was static with thoughts pinging here and there. Eventually, it quieted, and I fell into a restless sleep.

Chapter Ten

TUCKER

A few mornings later, I wasn't due to fly until the afternoon. I didn't mind those mornings at all because that meant I could lounge in the kitchen at the lodge and eat whatever Daphne was making, which was always good. This morning was made-to-order omelets.

"What do you want?" she asked, smiling over at me.

"Whatever you want to make."

"No, it's whatever you want."

"No, it's whatever you want because you know what's best," I countered.

"How about smoked salmon and goat cheese with some red peppers?"

"That sounds amazing."

"I've made it for you before," she said as

she rolled her eyes and promptly started making the omelet. She had this trick where she could crack two eggs at once. It was so cool.

"How do you do that?" I asked.

"Lots and lots of practice," she said dryly.

A few minutes later, after I was halfway through my omelet, I commented, "Don't take this the wrong way, but sometimes I'm jealous of Flynn."

Daphne smiled. "What do you mean?"

"I don't want the romance, but I want the food forever. He's got the food forever."

"As long as you work here, you've got the food," she said lightly.

I grinned. "True, and I don't plan to stop working here, so I guess I've got it all figured out."

She busied herself with cleaning up. Flynn popped into the kitchen for another mug of coffee, departing a moment later and calling over, "I gotta make some phone calls in the office."

"It's my office," Daphne called after him.

Flynn paused at the door, flashing a grin. "I won't use it when you need it, I promise." He winked and disappeared through the doorway into the hallway that led to their private apartment.

"That man," she said, the affection clear in her voice.

It was just Daphne and me now. She didn't mind silence, and I'd always liked that about her. She carried on doing whatever she was doing while I enjoyed my omelet and sipped my coffee.

"So, tell me about your life, Tucker," she said, startling me.

"You know about my life, Daphne. I live here. I fly. That's my life."

"I know, but you have a sister and family."

"Yup. Tori is a therapist. Every so often, she says she might move up here."

"Yeah, and your parents live in Arizona. How are they?"

"They're doing well. Happy and still together, so that's a win," I replied.

"Have you ever been in love?" she asked. Her tone was all light, but she didn't fool me.

That's why my spidey sense had been vibrating. "Maybe." I shrugged. I took the last bite of my omelet, eyeing her as I chewed. After I finished, I set down my fork. "Cut to the chase, Daphne. You want to know something, just ask."

She sighed. "Fine. Rumor has it you had a high school girlfriend, and something happened. I want to know what."

My heart thumped an achy beat. "Why?"

"Because I want you to be happy, and I feel like you won't let yourself, so I want to understand why."

"I am happy."

"Maybe, but you totally keep to yourself."

"So what? You don't need to play matchmaker for me. I swear to God I'm happy all by myself."

My mind flicked to that kiss with Skylar. That damn kiss had led to me avoiding her twice in the past few days. Because I flew planes and she worked nearby, I crossed paths with Skylar on the regular. "Why are you asking about high school?" I prompted.

"Because our first relationships often shape us," Daphne pointed out.

"Fine, I'll tell you." I just wanted to get this over with. "I had a girlfriend in high school. I loved her, the way you can love someone in high school." Even though it had been years, I had enough sense to know that once you were an adult, things were a little different when it came to love. "She died," I said flatly.

I'd said that so many times the words came out smooth, but there was still a dull throb of pain. Grief was weird. Sometimes, it faded, and other times, it was a looming shape in the darkness that swiped at you so hard you could barely breathe from the pain of it.

"Oh. I'm sorry," Daphne said softly.

"Yeah, me too. But I know you understand. You lost someone who mattered a lot, probably more than my high school girlfriend."

"That's not how it works. You can't compare losses."

I shrugged. "I really loved her, and life is really fucking unfair sometimes."

"Yeah, it is. Is that why you don't date?"

"Daphne," I warned. She simply shrugged, cocking her head to the side as she waited patiently for my answer.

"You know, shit happens," I finally said.

"Yeah, no shit," she said bluntly with her slight Southern twang. "Is that a reason to write love off for the rest of your life?"

"Look, my life is good. I don't really want to go through the love and loss thing again. Once is more than enough."

"I think taking that attitude about it actually makes it worse," she pointed out.

I didn't appreciate the defensive feeling that rose inside. She might have been right, but I didn't want to contemplate what that meant.

"Daphne," I warned again.

"What, Tucker? You kissed Skylar."

"Oh, for fuck's sake. Is that what this is all about?"

She shrugged, her lips twitching at the corners. "Maybe, maybe not. I like Skylar."

"Don't try to set us up. Don't even think about it. That kiss was a mistake. I don't know what I was thinking."

"Well, you obviously wanted to kiss her," she pointed out.

"Yeah, but Skylar is nice. She might have expectations, and I don't do expectations."

"Actually, I don't think she does."

"Why?" I pressed.

Daphne's eyes narrowed as she studied me. "I think she's more cynical than you."

Of course, because Daphne had the effect of tearing down my guard, I said, "She said a weird thing."

"What?"

"Don't ruin this, or something like that."

"Don't ruin what?" Daphne prompted.

"I don't know. She kind of keeps to herself. I don't know if she even has any friends."

"We're her friends," Daphne said loyally.

Daphne was a mother hen kind of soul. Once she decided someone was in her circle, she took them under her wing and protected them.

"You could ask her what she meant," she added.

"Uh, no, not gonna do that. I think it might be best if I just don't kiss her again. We can stay on friend turf."

Daphne rolled her eyes before her gaze sobered as she regarded me. "Take it from someone who went through a difficult loss. It's better to let yourself have something good afterward. It's almost like you earned it. Maybe if there's a little balance in the universe, you already paid the worst toll. Sometimes, I look around, and the people who don't go through the hard stuff don't have it figured out. After you've already loved and lost, you know how precious it is."

My heart gave an achy throb. At that moment, Cat came skipping into the kitchen, and our conversation was cut off. That was a huge fucking relief. I liked Daphne. Hell, I loved her the way I loved all my friends. But damn, she had hit some sore spots.

Chapter Eleven

SKYLAR

Work was busy. It was always busy, and I almost always had my headset on, but the comments the other night about Ludie and Dan potentially retiring had me wanting to eavesdrop. When the day wound down, I found myself lingering in the break room, if you could call it that.

The building had an open area out front where the cargo was temporarily stored at times and two offices down the hallway to the back. The larger one was where we had a big L-shaped desk with multiple computer monitors and the radio equipment to monitor and report scheduling. The small office belonged to Ludie. Dan didn't even have an office. He would linger in hers, sitting at the round table in the corner, or work in the break room.

I didn't know how to eavesdrop. I was terrible at it. I was also allergic to it. My years in foster care and the constancy of tolerating uncertainty had taught me the dangers of eavesdropping. Sometimes, you overheard the biological children complaining about you being there or conversations about what your social worker might do next as far as plans went. Long story short, it was much easier not to know at all.

I hated living with the uncertainty, but a toxic kind of uncertainty came with over-hearing conversations out of context. It was easier to wait for the shock of the truth when your social worker showed up and smiled to break the latest news about where you were going next.

Despite all that, I never forgot one of my social workers, Jolene. I loved Dolly Parton's song "Jolene," which really had nothing to do with this, solely because of the name. Jolene was the one who made sure Emily and I stayed in the same school system for years. She even tried to make sure we were in the same placements when she could after our first placement together, where we became besties.

Back to now, I was lingering in the break room until Dan passed by in the hallway and paused to glance at me curiously. "What the hell are you doing here this late, Skylar?" he asked in his usual, blunt, no-nonsense manner.

"Nothing," I said, trying to sound all casual.

He narrowed his eyes. "What's up? What do you need to know?"

"What do you mean?" I returned, feeling heat crawl up my neck and into my cheeks.

He came in and sat down. "You worried about Ludie retiring?" Dan had a mind-reading ability that startled me time and again.

"Yes." I surprised myself by answering honestly. I felt fidgety and rubbed the edge of my sleeve between my index finger and thumb.

"Don't worry, you're gonna keep your job."

"If she retires, what happens to the contract?" I asked. Their entire business revolved around having the transportation coordinating contract for the airport here.

Somehow, with his gruffness, Dan was easier than anyone to talk to. Not because he was warm and fuzzy, but because I could count on him to tell me the truth no matter how shitty it was. He shared that quality with Jolene. Although she was warm and fuzzy, she was relentlessly and bluntly honest. I appreciated that. I'd rather know the truth, even if it was a truth I didn't want to know.

"Talk to Ludie," Dan said.

"Now?"

"Sure."

I felt a little sick to my stomach as I stood. Crossing the hall, I walked directly into Ludie's office and stopped in front of her desk. She was staring at her computer, her hand on her mouse.

"Ludie?"

"Yes, sweetie?" she asked as her eyes lifted to mine.

"Are you retiring?"

"Someday," she said with a shrug.

"When?"

"Don't worry."

She'd literally ordered me to do the most impossible thing. I sighed. "Could you just tell me the plan for when you do? Not knowing the plan is really stressful for me."

"Sometimes, you just gotta go with the flow, sweetie."

I surprised myself by blurting out the truth. "Ludie, I grew up in foster care and was forced to go with the flow without any say in my situation for most of my life. This is the best job I've ever had, and I love it. If I'm going to lose my job because you retire, I'd rather know now."

"Sweetie, we'll set it up so we can transfer the contract to you," she said, her tone calm and her eyes warm.

"You will?"

"Sure."

"It's that simple?" I asked doubtfully.

She shrugged. "Well, it's not simple, and it means a lot more responsibility for you. I like you, and you do a really good job, so we'll make it work."

"That's it?" I never could stop with the questions.

"That's it."

"When are you retiring?"

She shrugged, and I wanted to scream.

She must've sensed my internal frustration. "Let's say in the next three years."

"So, I have three years to figure it out?"

"Well, you never know what might happen."

"Oh, my god, Ludie. Don't fuck with me."

At my exasperation, she grinned. "We'll make sure everything's lined out ahead of time."

"You've only known me since last summer. Why would you do this?"

"Because I like you. You're the first employee we've ever had. It's always just been Dan and me. We don't have kids. As I said, you're really good at your job."

"Oh." Considering I was on the verge of tears, that was all I could manage in response.

She smiled. "Susie talked to me."

"She did?!" I squeaked.

"Yeah, I was over at her mother's house. She mentioned that she'd help you do what you needed to do on the business end, and she will. Susie knows her shit. We'll have it all set up for when I'm ready to retire. Now, I've got to deal with ordering office supplies, so get out of here. Your shift is over. Plus, it's getting dark out."

I laughed to myself as I started driving home. As soon as I got over being dazed at Ludie's response, I immediately started worrying about how I was going to handle all of it. I was a world-class worrier. My favorite therapist called it anticipatory anxiety. She told me my chaotic childhood had set me up to be constantly on guard for what could go wrong. Life had taught me that something *always* went wrong. I'd had one stable figure in my life, and she died.

Every time I thought of that therapist, I wondered what she would think if she knew Emily had died. I thought she would feel sad for me, which rankled because I didn't want anyone to feel sad on my behalf. I blinked back the tears that stung my eyes and took a deep breath.

Chapter Twelve

SKYLAR

The following morning, I rolled to a stop in the gravel parking area at Red Truck Coffee, smiling when I saw Cammi through the serving window. My boots crunched on the gravel as I walked over to get in the back of the line.

It was brisk this morning, and I found it amazing that she was already busy. Among the other subjects covered at dinner the other night with the girls, I'd learned the business picked up here almost as soon as she opened every spring because of the tourist traffic. In my short time here, I'd learned to pick out the tourists from the locals. The tourists usually wore more expensive clothing, while those heading to the harbor for fishing usually wore battered jeans or Carhartts and rubber boots.

I'd only been waiting for a few moments when someone else arrived behind me. I glanced over my shoulder to find Tucker. "Oh!" I squeaked.

He'd been looking at something on his phone and lifted his eyes to mine. "Oh, hey, Skylar."

"Hey, sorry to interrupt."

He smiled, shrugging. "Just looking at my flight schedule for the day."

"That's on your phone?"

"We have a shared calendar. Nora makes sure we all stay on top of it," he explained. "How's it going?"

"Oh, fine. You?"

"Pretty good."

Things felt tense, and I felt confused. I wish we hadn't kissed. I thought it was going to ruin everything just like I'd feared. I wanted to make friends here. Romance was a disaster for me, and I knew this thoroughly. I couldn't get my body to understand my instructions. I never could. It was worse with Tucker than it had ever been with anybody.

He was so freaking handsome and sexy. His brown curls were rumpled, and blue eyes were so bright in the early morning light. He carried himself with ease, and I doubted he even really knew he was handsome. Or, perhaps he did. Considering I'd cast all reservations aside and kissed him without a care in the world when I definitely knew better, I didn't doubt he was accustomed to women throwing themselves at him.

"You headed into work?" he asked. I nodded. He lifted his chin, nudging it forward. "You're up."

"Oh!" I squeaked again, turning and hurrying to the counter. "Hey, Cammi," I said as soon as I got there, willing my cheeks to cool.

I was a blusher of the worst kind. Fortunately, it was Cammi. Even if she hadn't been friendly and invited me to dinner the other night, I knew she wasn't the kind of person to tease. Not in front of others. She was simply nice, the nicest, really.

"Good morning, Skylar. Do you want to try something new? I have a new thing."

"What's that?"

"It's a double shot espresso with my new syrup."

"What kind of syrup?" I asked suspiciously.

"I promise it's not too sweet," she said with a warm smile.

"You know me. I definitely don't like a lot of sweet in my coffee," I said, shaking my head quickly.

"I know. You want to try it?"

"Let's do it."

"Do you need anything for food? Daphne delivered orange cranberry scones, which are completely amazing, and savory pinwheels. Today we have spinach and swiss, or ham and swiss. Take your pick."

"I'll have one of the scones and a spinach pinwheel. I need both sweet and savory this morning."

"I'll take both too," Tucker said from my side.

I practically jumped at the sound of his voice. Scooting to the side, I created some distance between us. "I can get yours this morning," he added.

"No need." Apparently, all I could do was squeak whenever I spoke to Tucker this morning.

"You can get mine next time," he pressed.

"I've never seen you here," I blurted out.

"Yeah, well, Cammi just opened for this season a few weeks ago. Trust me. You will see me here almost every freaking day. This is where I get my coffee on the way in."

"You don't have coffee out at the lodge?" I asked.

"Daphne is amazing with food, but Cammi's coffee is better," Tucker said simply.

Cammi smiled warmly. "Thank you. I know what your usual is." She winked before she turned around and began prepping our drinks.

"What's your usual?" I asked.

"A shot in the dark."

"What's that?"

"Her dark coffee with a shot of espresso. I need the caffeine to last me all day since I'll be in the air."

"How late do you fly?"

"Until it's too dark to be in the sky. Nora's got me landing at—" He lifted his phone, tapping the screen and scrolling with his thumb. "Five-thirty. Just before sunset. She switched it up so I can go to yoga class out at the lodge."

"Because it's good for you," Cammi called over.

"Who covers your later flights that day?"

"Trey Holden."

He was referring to an attorney and an occasional pilot who I'd only met once when he stopped by to drop off a delivery for a client across the bay. "Oh, right. He flies for you all sometimes. It's nice you all have the yoga class out at the lodge. I've gone to Gemma's class a few times in town. She's great."

"Here's your coffee, Skylar," Cammi called, sliding the paper cup across the counter to me.

Tucker slapped down a bill when I started to pull my wallet out. I felt uncertain. This was a thing I did not know how to handle. Even before I'd cut dating out of my life, I'd preferred to pay for everything. I didn't want to rely on anyone for anything.

"Tucker," I warned.

"Skylar, trust me. I get coffee for all my friends. We trade off all the time."

"He does," Cammi said when she handed over his coffee.

She gave Tucker his change, which he stuffed in the tip jar. He stepped to the side while she took the orders for the next in line. She started prepping their coffees and then called our names to hand over our scones and savories in two different paper bags.

I was standing there, wondering what to say next, so I sipped my coffee. "Thank you," I finally said.

"You're up tomorrow." He threw me a grin, and my belly shimmied.

"Are you sure I'm going to see you?"

"If not tomorrow, soon. Next time you see me, you're up. How's that?"

"All right." I didn't wait and bolted across the parking lot, quickly getting in my car and taking a gulp from my coffee. I shouldn't have been this flustered, but it was all because of that stupid kiss. I took a deep breath and started driving. Only moments later, I realized Tucker was right behind me. Of course, he was going to the same place.

"Fuck, fuck, fuck," I muttered.

He was probably going to park right beside me. I would just ignore him.

Chapter Thirteen

TUCKER

I followed Skylar to the airport, telling myself it was no big deal that it felt like my body had been lit on fire simply by standing near her. This reaction would pass. It had to.

Of course, I also hadn't forgotten that kiss and kept wondering what Skylar meant when she told me not to ruin it.

I ended up parking right beside her because it was the natural place to park. It was directly across from one of the hangars for Walker Adventures. Not to mention, there weren't very many parking spots. I found myself waiting at the back of her car.

She climbed out, asking, "Has anyone noticed my cargo thing?"

I chuckled. "Nope. I told you nobody was

going to notice. Honestly, by the time someone notices, they'll think it was there all along."

Skylar eyed me dubiously. "If it's a problem, let me know."

"It's not going to be a problem."

She nodded and took a swallow of coffee.

"What did you mean when you said don't ruin this?" My question slipped out.

Her eyes went wide, and she sputtered on a swallow of coffee. She yanked a tissue out of her purse and wiped the coffee off her chin. "Why did you do that?" she demanded.

"I was just asking a question."

"Your timing was really bad. Don't ask awkward questions when someone just took a sip of something," she muttered.

"Point taken." I waited.

A few beats ticked by, and she replied, "Nothing."

"Nothing?"

"Forget the kiss. Forget what I said." Her words rushed out.

Before I had a chance to say anything else, she turned and actually ran across the parking lot, disappearing a moment later through the door into the building where she worked.

Even though I wanted to follow her, I

didn't. I knew Ludie and Dan would be there. There was nowhere to ask her that question privately. Considering her response, I suppose I'd have to take it for what it was.

My day was busy, which was a good thing. It kept my mind occupied. Except twice, Skylar's throaty, melodic voice came through the radio. The sound slid like lava through my veins. There was no way I was going to forget that kiss.

I pondered Daphne's comments the other day and wondered.

Chapter Fourteen

SKYLAR

After the last plane landed that day, it started drizzling, and I cursed the sky. I had an appointment for my car, and I was supposed to drop it off tonight at the mechanic shop. Whatever.

Ludie and Dan had already left for the day. I closed up shop and raced over to the mechanic shop, dropping off my keys, signing for my car, and hurrying out. It was maybe a fifteen-minute walk to my apartment from here. I could make it, and the rain would be on my side.

About five minutes into my walk, the sky opened, and the equivalent of a bucket was dumped onto me. I was drenched within seconds. I tightened my jacket around my shoulders pointlessly and lowered my head as I walked into the rain, ignoring the cars that drove by.

I kept telling myself the walk really wasn't that far. I heard the sound of a vehicle approaching from behind and then slowing. I kept my face trained on the pavement in front of me, watching as the rain struck the surface and water splashed up.

"Skylar!" a voice called through the din.

I couldn't help it. I ended up looking to the side. It was Tucker. Fuck.

"Get in," he ordered.

"I'm fine. I'm just walking home."

"It's pouring. Get in the truck," he pressed.

"Really, it's okay," I lied because I was miserable and soaking wet and freezing cold.

I was also insanely stubborn about being independent and not needing anyone for anything. I certainly didn't need a ride in the rain. I could handle the walk.

"Either you get in, or I'm driving five miles an hour beside you, all the way back to your place," he called through the rain.

He couldn't see my face well, but I rolled my eyes and sighed. When I started to pull my hands out of my pockets, I realized they were already at the point of numbness where they didn't even work very well. My hand slipped when I reached for the door handle. He pushed the door open from the inside.

I scrambled in, slamming the door shut and sitting there, feeling like a drowned kitten.

"What the hell, Skylar?" Tucker demanded.

His truck was warm and dry inside. I couldn't even talk over the chattering of my teeth. He turned the heat up, blasting it at top speed and angling every vent along the dashboard in my direction.

"Next time you need a ride somewhere, just text me. If I'm not in the air, I'll come pick you up."

"I wa-wa-wa-was f-f-f-f-ine." I managed to get three words out through my chattering teeth. I finally risked a glance at him, expecting to see annoyance.

He simply looked concerned. "You're freezing, Skylar. Why are you walking home when you have a car?"

Shivering, I took a breath. "I scheduled an appointment for maintenance. There's a recall, and they told me it was essential." The heat was filtering through enough I could speak.

"And you just walked home, and you're

going to walk into work tomorrow?" he asked as he put his truck into gear and began driving.

"It's not that far," I protested.

"You know, this isn't about you being a woman. I just want to make that point first. I am all about walking when you can enjoy the fresh air and the amazing view. But for fuck's sake, it's awful out. If Ludie finds out you didn't ask her for a ride, she is going to give you some hell."

"Well, she won't know as long as you don't tell her," I managed to retort. Although I sounded kind of ridiculous because my teeth were still chattering between every word.

Tucker trained his eyes on the road and drove. The rain was coming down so fast his windshield was a blur of water, and the wipers could barely keep up. He gestured toward it as if reading my mind. "It's fucking pouring out."

"Obviously, I know that." I uncurled my hands and held them in front of the heater. I was shaking all over.

"You live above Midnight Sun Arts Gallery, right?"

"Yeah, thank you for stopping."

"Anytime. You only owe me one thing in return."

Disappointment pierced me. I was used to people who always wanted something, but I hadn't thought Tucker was like that. "Next time you need a ride, tell me. Short notice, in advance, whatever. That's all I ask."

"Sure," I lied.

He wouldn't know when I needed a ride. I would just lie about it. Only minutes later, Tucker came to a stop in front of the gallery, glancing my way. "I'll walk you up."

"I don't need—" I began.

He shook his head. "Oh, no, I'm walking you up. I'm still afraid you're on the verge of hypothermia."

I didn't even have it in me to argue. I was too cold and wet. Moments later, we were standing in the hallway, and I was dripping water all over the floor. I couldn't get my hands to make my key fit in the lock.

After the third try, Tucker said, "Let me try."

The brush of his hand against mine when he took the keys from me was warm, and his voice was gruff. Mere seconds later, we were in my apartment, and he looked at me.

"I'm worried you're hypothermic."

"I'm not." I tried to sound insistent, but when your teeth were chattering, nothing came out very well.

"I'm not leaving until you're showered and dry, and you're not shivering," he said flatly.

"Are you serious?" I sputtered, still shivering from head to toe.

"That, or I'm taking you into the hospital."

"What?!" That galvanized me, and I threw my wet jacket off.

He caught it deftly and hung it on the coat rack by the door. He rested his hands on his hips as he arched a brow and looked at me.

"Oh, my god," I muttered.

I turned and walked directly into the bathroom. It felt weird to have him here, so I closed the door and locked it. Even when I was alone, I locked my bathroom door. That was a habit from my foster care days.

I was trembling all over as I peeled my clothes off. The relief that came when the steaming water ran over me was profound. I didn't know if I really was bordering on hypothermia, but it took several minutes before I was actually warm in that shower. I finally felt a sense of relief and could actually hold the soap in my hand.

I didn't know how long I was in the shower because my phone was in my coat pocket, which was out in the living room. I had my composure back by the time I was done.

I toweled off only to discover I didn't have any dry clothes in here. Fuck. I snagged my robe off the hook on the wall, a thick, terry cloth robe. I shrugged into it and belted it tightly. It was actually Emily's and came all the way down to my ankles. I felt sheepish as I stepped out of the bathroom.

Tucker was looking at his phone where he sat on a chair at the small table in the kitchen. He glanced up, his eyes scanning over me. "You look warmer."

I figured my skin was already flushed. Thank goodness because the mere sound of his voice sent a wash of heat through me. "I am. I don't know if I was hypothermic, but thank you for the ride home. I was freezing, and it took longer than I expected to warm up in that shower."

He smiled, just barely. "I've been hypothermic. I don't know if you were either, but I know the signs. This kind of weather is the worst for it."

"It is?" I crossed over and fetched my phone out of my coat pocket.

"Yeah. More people die of hypothermia in the spring and fall than in the middle of the winter. People are usually more prepared for the cold in the winter."

"Oh. I didn't know that. I grew up in California. It's not very cold there."

"I think you should eat next," he said.

"I can feed myself," I muttered, feeling defensive.

He studied me quietly. "I checked your fridge. You have half a carton of milk and two eggs. How about I order some pizza?"

I opened my mouth to argue, but he beat me to it. "I'm not leaving until you're fed."

"Jesus, you're bossy. I'm gonna get dressed."

I flounced out of the room if one can flounce with wet hair and a robe that's too big.

I closed and locked my bedroom door. I quickly pulled on a pair of clean, dry sweatpants and a giant fleece top. I was going for my most comfortable and most baggy option. Hopefully, also unattractive. That was my entire goal.

A moment later, I took a deep breath in front of my bedroom door before walking out. I could handle this. Tucker was just being a nice guy.

"What kind of pizza would you like?" he asked as soon as I appeared.

"Whatever you want."

"We can get whatever I want, but what do *you* want?"

That was another habit that Emily used to give me hell about. When you're in foster care, you try to make yourself as small and as unobtrusive as possible. You didn't want any of your needs or wants to be too much. So, if a family liked pizza with green peppers and onions, which I hated, by the way, you just went with it, and you didn't pick it off either.

"Um, I like bacon and pineapple or lots of mushrooms."

The second Tucker smiled, my belly went a little insane, practically doing gymnastics inside, and my pulse galloped off wildly, kicking and bucking.

"Let's do half and half. I like bacon and pineapple, and I'll eat mushrooms too."

"You don't have to eat mushrooms. Let's just get bacon and pineapple," I said quickly.

"Nope. You said you like mushrooms, so you're gonna get the best of both worlds."

Another second later, he was on the phone ordering. He also ordered breadsticks and an extra bacon and pineapple pizza. As soon as he hung up, I said, "There's no way we can eat all that."

"I'll bring the leftovers out to the lodge. Everyone will love it," he said easily.

I didn't like this feeling, but I felt a tiny pang of jealousy. Even though I knew they were all friends, they felt like a family. It was the kind of place I'd always wanted in my life, where everybody cared about each other and teased each other. A place where you could have faith you'd be welcome. It was safe.

Brushing those thoughts away, I nodded. "Do you want something to drink?" I asked.

"Water will do. I'm not a fan of milk," he teased.

My cheeks got hot as I sighed. "I haven't been to the store lately. I'm not the greatest about shopping. I usually just pick up something from the deli at the grocery store."

"Well, you better not tell Daphne, or she'll insist that you come out for dinner every night."

"Oh, I can't do that," I said quickly.

"You could, and it would be fine," Tucker said, his gaze entirely serious.

Chapter Fifteen

TUCKER

Skylar's eyes held mine. I wished I knew how to read her expression. I sensed she was nervous, but she had perfected the art of giving nothing away.

She stared at me steadily for a few beats before she shrugged. "I kind of doubt that."

Her matter-of-fact tone twisted my heart. She wasn't even being sarcastic.

"Don't," I said, my tone low. I needed to make her understand. "Believe me."

"Tucker—" She rolled her eyes. "You barely know me, and Daphne barely knows me. It was really nice that she invited me out, but—"

"Skylar, most of us see you almost every

day and hear your voice all the time. I kissed you."

As soon as I said that, I wanted to snatch it back. Not because I was hiding something, but it wasn't the time for this detour in the conversation.

"That kiss was a mistake," she said flatly.

Her cheeks went pink as she turned away. She crossed over to a cabinet and fetched two glasses, filling them each with water. "Do you want some ice?" she asked over her shoulder.

"No, thanks."

"I can make some tea," she offered as she turned.

"I'm not really a tea guy."

"Hot chocolate?"

"Okay, I'll go for hot chocolate," I replied. I really could go for a beer, but I had to drive home.

She filled a kettle with water and put it on the stove before turning on the burner. "We're not going to kiss again." She turned around, her words coming out almost forcefully. She followed that with, "I have to check on my guinea pigs." She hurried across the room, stopping beside a table beyond the couch where I saw there were three connecting glass containers.

I followed her over, watching as she cooed to two chubby guinea pigs, one black and white, and the other brown and white. She checked their water before turning to face me. "This is Pigley." She gestured to the black and white one. "And this is Squiggly."

"They're cute," I offered.

She smiled a little and then turned to walk back into the kitchen.

"Why can't we kiss again?" I was determined not to let her avoid that topic.

"Because it's a bad idea." Her eyes narrowed, and her chin pointed forward.

"Was kissing me that bad?" I teased.

Her eyes went wide, and she sputtered on a sip of water. She swallowed and shook her head. "No!"

Now, we were already in deep on the topic, so I just went for it. "Tell me what you meant when you said, 'Don't ruin this.'"

She surprised me by even answering. "I'm trying to make a life here, and I don't want to screw it up. Relationships mess things up."

"It was just a kiss, Skylar."

"I know. It's nothing."

I didn't know what was happening to me, but I knew I was being crazy. I had loved someone and watched her die way too young. I'd told myself love was never worth it again.

I wasn't kidding myself into thinking I was in love with Skylar. Yet she was really getting under my skin. It rankled me that she was opposed to a kiss.

"That kiss wasn't nothing. It was a good kiss," I insisted.

Her flush deepened. I sensed she wanted to stay all the way across the kitchen from me. She crossed the kitchen and sat down in the only other chair at an angle across from me. She was maybe a foot away now.

"Fine. It was a good kiss," she muttered.

I felt my lips tug into a smile. "Was it that bad?"

"I just told you it was good," she insisted.

"I think we should try again. I have a point to make."

"Oh, my fucking god," she muttered, rolling her eyes. "You do *not* have a point to make. I'm starting to make friends. I don't want to kiss you and have it ruin the friends I have."

"Kissing me won't ruin that."

"How do you know?"

"What the hell happened to you, Skylar?" I heard myself asking.

Her eyes went wide. For just a second, I could've sworn she was about to burst into tears. It passed so fast I doubted it, yet it didn't change the feeling I sensed—an intense sadness and loss.

"My parents are both dead, my mother from an overdose and my father from a fight in jail. I spent most of my childhood in foster care until I 'aged out,'" she offered with air quotes. "That's what happens when you don't have your own family. Most people don't really care, and it doesn't really matter once you turn eighteen. I don't count on anybody but myself. I came to Alaska because I was supposed to move here with my best friend. She was the only person I called family. We ended up in foster care together. It was actually a good home, but then the foster mom got sick, so we had to move. I had a good social worker who ensured we stayed in the same school district, even if we couldn't be in the same home. Emily and I planned this trip. She found this apartment." Skylar paused, sweeping her arm in an arc. "We even got jobs, and then she died. My car is our car. Her name is still on the title with mine. I don't even know what I'm supposed to do about that."

She spoke calmly as if she had practiced every word. The emotion underneath reverberated like a drumbeat. I just wanted to wrap her in my arms and shield her from anything else going wrong in her life. Because nobody deserved that shit.

She lifted her chin, ending with, "So you see why I don't really count on anything or anyone."

"I do," I said quietly. "I really do."

I reached over and tugged her chair close to mine, bracing my knees around hers. "I know what it means to lose someone you love. I do have family, and they were there for me. I'm sorry you don't."

This conversational detour had turned into a new highway at this point. One that I sensed led directly into the very heart of Skylar. My own heart was thumping hard and fast. We stared at each other quietly. I lifted a hand and brushed a few drying locks of hair off her cheeks.

I didn't plan to kiss her. I wasn't thinking very well, or at all. The moment her plush lips opened underneath mine, I angled my head to the side and let out a groan. She arched into me, and our kiss went on and on and on. I drank her in. She tasted sweet and warm. The next thing I knew, I had tugged her onto my lap. She was a warm bundle of softness and curves. She straddled me, and her hands cupped my cheeks as she took over our kiss.

It spiraled out of my control, snapping the tether of my control loose. Fuck me. She kissed with abandon. Our tongues tangled while her hips rocked over the hard ridge of my arousal. She felt a little wild in my arms. I had one arm curled around her waist, and I couldn't resist sliding the other under the hem of her soft, inviting top. Her skin was silky and warm under my touch, still dewy from her shower. She pressed into my touch when I cupped her breast. Her nipple was tight, the weight of her breast lush and full.

I broke free, gulping in air as she rasped my name. I knew what I needed to do. "Just let me do this," I murmured against her throat.

I was fully prepared for her to tell me to fuck right the hell off. She didn't.

This side of Skylar was one I'd never seen. She felt vulnerable with an edge of wildness to her. I couldn't have imagined her like this if she wasn't right here in my lap, alive and vibrating. I could feel the need emanating from her.

I reached between us. Her eyes were wide, watching me as I watched her. I slipped my hand into her sweatpants to discover she wasn't even wearing underwear. My cock throbbed. I delved into the core of her. Her arousal slicked my fingers as I explored her folds.

She still watched, biting her bottom lip. I couldn't help it. I needed to taste her. Dipping my head, I dragged my tongue along her collarbone, dropping a hot kiss in the divot at the base of her throat. She cried out when I sank my fingers into her. She surprised me, coming abruptly and letting out a noisy cry. Her channel clenched around my fingers, and wetness drenched my hand. I stayed with her through it until she relaxed against me. She curled soft into my shoulder as I slowly drew my touch away. I was stunned by the intimacy of the moment. I had to have more. I needed to know her. I needed to show her that it could be worth it.

I kept expecting her to bolt out of my lap, but she didn't. After a few moments, she lifted her head, and we studied each other quietly.

She took a breath before saying, "You promised it wouldn't ruin anything."

"I meant it," I said just as the doorbell rang.

The sound snapped through the moment. She scrambled off my lap then, hurrying to the door. She greeted the pizza delivery guy and gave me a moment to stand, adjust my jeans, and wash my hands in the sink. I crossed to the door, saying over her shoulder, "I've got it."

The delivery guy held up the boxes. "Perfect. Twenty bucks even."

I pulled out forty and told him to keep the change. Skylar's eyes were wide when I closed the door. "Why did you give him such a big tip?" she yelped.

"Because the weather sucks, and he probably gets paid minimum wage. Tips are what help him get by."

She eyed me and shrugged. "Maybe you have a point."

I shrugged. "It's my money."

She kind of glared at me and then walked back into the kitchen. "Are you staying or going?" she called as she reached to get plates out of a cabinet.

"I said I was staying until you ate, so I'm staying."

"But the pizza will get cold by the time you get home."

"No one will care. Reheated pizza is perfect."

I was frankly starving myself. What I'd allowed to happen a few minutes ago wasn't supposed to happen. Yet I couldn't undo what happened.

I was going to have to find a way forward, find a way to convince her—even though this was fucking insane for me to consider—we had something between us worth exploring.

After all of her skittishness, Skylar was calm after that. She handed me a plate, re-filled my water, and made hot chocolate from packets. She sat down across from me, putting two slices of pizza on her plate. We ate quietly, and then she pushed her plate away.

I met her eyes. "Let's give this a chance."

Chapter Sixteen

SKYLAR

"Excuse me?"

"Us," Tucker replied.

"No way."

He eyed me for a long moment while my heart thudded madly. "We'll talk about it later," he finally said.

I shrugged, relieved he'd decided to let it go. I considered it a small miracle I was marginally keeping my shit together. "I've eaten. You can go now."

He insisted on rinsing off his plate, but he left, and I managed to say good night and thank him for the ride again. After he was gone, I plunked down on the couch. I curled my knees up to my chest, resting my chin on them as I stared out into the rainy darkness.

The lights cast from the docks in the harbor glimmered in a blur. I could see the ocean's surface rippling underneath the rain. I'd asked Tucker not to ruin it. And now, I had probably ruined it.

Taking a deep breath, I tried to calm down inside. My body was still pinging with sensations. I'd gone and done the stupidest thing ever and flung myself into that kiss, into *all* of that, with him.

Romance was so dangerous for me because I tended to fling myself into it. It was easier to think it didn't matter if it was just sex. Ugh. That was so stupid.

Restless, I took another shower, trying to forget the way Tucker's hands felt on my body. God. It felt so good to be in his arms. I would have to talk to him again and explain that I'd kind of lost my mind there.

The universe granted me a small favor, and I fell asleep. The following morning, I headed for Misty Mountain Café, purposely avoiding Red Truck Coffee because Tucker might be there. I liked the café in equal measure. It was ridiculously early. The sun was just cresting the horizon as I walked down the road to pick up my car. The morning had that freshly washed look. The rain had stopped, and the sky was awash in color—a deep red with tangerine and gold shaded through it and angling upward. The air was bracing and pure.

When I heard a vehicle slowing behind me, I cursed. I forgot Tucker knew I had to walk to pick up my car. I steeled myself for him to slow and stop beside me. When I risked a glance at the vehicle, the window was rolling down, and it wasn't him. It was Daphne.

"Hey, Skylar," she greeted me. "Pretty morning for a walk. You probably don't need a ride, but maybe you do." Her auburn hair was twisted in a braid on top of her head, and her smile was bright.

"It is beautiful, and I wouldn't mind a ride," I replied, deciding to be brave.

She reached across, opening the door to her SUV. "Hop in."

"Where are you going?" she asked.

"I need to pick up my car. Do you mind dropping me off?"

"How about we get coffee together, and then I take you to your car?"

I hesitated. Old habits die hard and all that. "Sure," I heard myself saying.

Coffee with Daphne would be nice. I heard Emily's voice in my mind. *"You have to*

*make friends. We both do. We'll go somewhere new,
and our life won't be tangled up in the past."*

"Are you delivering food this morning?" I
asked.

"Nope. Tucker had an early flight today.
He's already dropped off this morning's delivery to Cammi."

I bit my tongue. I wanted to ask where he
was flying, but there were only so many options, and it really was none of my business.
Plus, I'd learn the answer as soon as I got
into the office this morning. We kept a log of
all the flights to coordinate cargo transport
on the fly if we needed it.

Daphne commented on the weather and
laughed about something that happened in
the kitchen at the lodge. Within minutes, we
were at Misty Mountain Café. We walked in
together, and I realized this was the first time
I'd gone somewhere together with anyone
since Emily died.

That was how pathetic my life was. One
friend was gone. I ignored the grief that
stung in my throat, relieved only one couple
was in front of us in the line. Daphne was
eyeing the bakery case. As soon as we
reached the counter, she asked, "Cammi, did
Tucker come by?"

"Of course, he did. I just haven't had time to put everything out."

Daphne glanced around the café. "No one else is waiting. Let's do it now," she said.

"I'll help," I offered.

Seconds later, the three of us were in the kitchen, and I looked around. A long table through the center of the room had trays covering half of it. Cammi passed up trays in order, and I carried them to the front, handing the scones and savories to Daphne as she carefully organized them in the display case.

"What do you want for coffee?" Cammi asked as we worked.

Daphne called over, "I'll take a mocha, not skinny."

"Can I have the dark chocolate one?" I asked.

Cammi started prepping our drinks and refused to let us pay. "Are you sure?" Daphne pressed.

"Yes, you just did some work for me. Easily five bucks apiece."

Daphne rolled her eyes, and we both stuffed the money we would have spent on our coffee in the tip jar. "You know, I pay my staff really well," Cammi commented. "You don't have to tip. Do you want anything for breakfast?"

"I need a scone and a savory, and I'll pay for those," I said.

Cammi rolled her eyes but didn't argue that point. Daphne, of course, had already had breakfast. "What did you guys have this morning? According to Elias, your breakfasts are legendary," she commented.

"Legendary?" Daphne's cheeks pinkened slightly.

"He says your omelets are to die for. Honestly, I'd love to come out there for breakfast, but I don't think I can bring myself to get there early enough, not to mention I have to be either here or at the truck early," Cammi explained.

"What time do you start work?" I asked.

"Both places open at five, so I'm at one or the other."

"Whoa, and I thought I was an early riser," I offered.

She shrugged slightly. "It's a coffee place. Plus, in the summer, tourists are headed out to fish, pilots are headed to the sky, and the fishermen are hitting the docks early."

"Is it hard to find staff?" Daphne inquired.

"You'd be shocked, but no. People like it.

It's good pay, not to mention that they finish their day early. The truck closes by two. Here, I have the evening shift, but that's a different crew." Just then, a crush of people came in, and Cammi waved us off.

Anxiety spun in tiny circles in my chest when I sat down across from Daphne. She was all relaxed, which made me hyperaware that I wasn't. We sipped coffee quietly, and I took a few bites of my spinach pinwheel.

"I just wanted to say, I know a little something about starting over," she began.

"You do?" Her comment startled me enough that I forgot to stay quiet.

She nodded. "I came here on vacation. I don't know if you could call spending a month at a lodge in almost the middle of nowhere a vacation, but my plan was to do something completely new and different. My son had just died."

"Oh!" My palm flew to my chest. "I am *so* sorry."

"It's okay. I don't know what happened to you, but my gut tells me something hard happened. You don't need to tell me, but I get it. It's hard to start over. Sometimes, when the worst thing happens, and you make it through to the other side, you actually are stronger." Her words were clear, and her eyes warm and understanding.

Before I could think, I simply spoke the truth. "My best friend died. She was really the only person who was family to me."

"I'm sorry," Daphne said solemnly.

I knew she really meant it. I was amazed I didn't burst into tears even though my throat was tight. "Thank you. Trying to make new friends is kind of difficult."

"Right? It's fucking hard to make friends as a grown-up," she said bluntly.

Hearing Daphne say fucking made me laugh.

"What's so funny?"

"I don't know. You're just so put together, and I didn't expect you to swear."

"I swear like a sailor." She grinned.

"So you didn't plan to stay here then?"

"Oh, god no." Her eyes went wide as she shook her head. "I fell in love. But first, Flynn ran off one of their cooks, and they were shorthanded, so I offered to help. We fell in love. I wouldn't change a thing. You already have a job, though, so I'm guessing you plan to stay."

I shrugged. "Emily and I were supposed to come together. We both found jobs."

"What was she going to do?"

"She was going to wait tables and finish her flight training. She died from complications from her injuries in a plane accident the week before we were supposed to come here," I explained, the words coming out smooth by some miracle.

"Oh, no," Daphne breathed.

"I know." I swallowed. "I want to try to fly in a small plane. Just for her. But I'm scared." I couldn't believe how open I was with Daphne, but she had a way about her that made it easy.

"You'll know when the time is right," Daphne said sagely.

I believed her.

I took a few more bites of my savory as we fell quiet.

"Tucker's a really nice guy," she said, just after I thought she was nice for enjoying the silence.

My cheeks immediately burned with heat. "Sure, he is," I said, trying to sound all casual.

"He really *is* a nice guy. He's not a player or anything. I'm not usually into matchmaking, if you're wondering."

"Matchmaking?" I repeated. My brain wasn't firing on all cylinders between my embarrassment and this whole freaking conversation.

"You know, somebody who tries to set people up. I'm not trying to set you up, but I have a feeling about you and Tucker, and I just thought you should know."

I internally sighed, thinking about the feel of his fingers inside me last night. I was glad I had clothes on, so Daphne couldn't see I was blushing all over.

"Oh," I managed.

"Don't forget, I know about the kiss," she whispered conspiratorially as she leaned across the table with a sly but understanding glint in her eyes.

I almost choked. I managed to keep chewing and took a sip of coffee before I braved a look over at her. "Who else knows about the kiss?"

"You know. Nora told you she was walking to her house and saw you."

"Oh, my god," I groaned. I leaned forward, dropping my face in my hands and sighing. I'd conveniently put that conversation away in my brain from the other night.

Lifting my head, I let my hands fall before lifting my coffee mug and taking a fortifying swallow. "I'm so embarrassed."

"Why? It's a kiss. You're an adult. He's an adult. Plus, he's adorable. Those brown curls and those blue eyes." She grinned.

I sighed again. "He is."

"You don't know me that well yet, so you're probably not going to have enough nerve to ask nosy questions. I'll just tell you everything I know. Tucker has been flying with Walker Adventures for four years. He, Flynn, Elias, Diego, and Gabriel are friends from the Air Force, where they all flew together. When Flynn came home to take care of Nora, Cat, and Grant after their mom died, he needed pilots, so they all came. They really are like family. Tucker is totally loyal. He stays in touch with his parents and his sister in Arizona. There, that's everything I know about Tucker. He hasn't had a serious relationship since high school that I know of, but he's not a casual kind of guy. He's loyal, trustworthy, and good as gold."

"Wow. You just told me a lot," I said, kind of in awe.

"Well, I knew you weren't going to ask," she said pointedly.

"I might have," I muttered before taking a bite of my pinwheel and chewing.

"I wouldn't have had the nerve," she replied. "I think you should give him a chance."

I laughed, still blushing. "I'll think about it."

She nodded, studying me for a moment. "Maybe I'm totally off base, but I just figured I'd tell you. If there was one thing I wish the universe would do, it would be to give us a real-life guardian angel who told us everything. Like when I came to Alaska, I was scared to death and totally had the hots for Flynn. I wish somebody had told me it would work out, and it would be okay."

"Well, could you tell me that?"

Daphne cast me a sheepish smile. "Actually, no, I can't promise that. I just have a good feeling."

I laughed, trying to mask my anxiety about all of this—the kiss, Tucker, trying to make friends. Daphne was gracious enough to let the topic drop after that.

Cammi stopped by our table before we left to chat. When Daphne dropped me off to pick up my car a little bit later, I was smiling. Maybe I could make friends. Perhaps I could find my fresh start. But Daphne having a feeling about Tucker and me? That seemed a little insane.

Chapter Seventeen

SKYLAR

Work was busy, but it was always busy. I liked being busy. An upside to growing up in foster care and chaos was gratitude for some basic things. Having a job, staying busy, and being able to pay my bills was so amazing. I loved being able to take care of myself, and I was so profoundly grateful I could.

All of that to say, I managed not to obsess about Tucker all day. I was too busy. It was all good until I was walking out to my car at the end of the day to find him leaning in the back of his truck. I prayed he wouldn't notice me, but the gods decided to have a little fun at my expense.

I stayed on the far side, maybe twenty feet away, between the rows of vehicles. Just as I got close, he lifted his head and closed the cab of his truck, turning immediately. "Hey, Skylar."

"Hey," I practically yelped.

He leaned his hips against the back of his truck. It was then I realized my car was right beside his truck. I wasn't even paying attention this morning when I parked, probably because I was still so flustered from my conversation with Daphne. Being reminded that she and Nora and Lord knows who else knew about the kiss had left me disconcerted. Of course, only Tucker knew about last night, so I hoped he would keep that quiet.

I got hot all over with my skin tingling and butterflies twirling in my belly.

"Your car all taken care of?" he asked.

"Yep," I squeaked.

"I was going to stop and see if you needed a ride, but I had to be in early this morning."

I nodded, realizing I was standing there like an idiot on the other side of the parking lot. I took a deep breath and tried to walk casually over to him, stuffing my hands in my pockets on the way. "How were your flights today?"

"Good." His voice was all rumbly and sexy.

"You busy today?"

"It's always busy."

We stared at each other. He opened his mouth to say something, but I beat him to it, blurting out, "Can we forget about last night?"

He studied me, and I felt as if he could see right inside my heart. It was as if he found a secret door I didn't know existed, and he'd already broken the lock.

"I know you want me to say yes," he said carefully before pausing. "But I'd be lying. How about let's not do that because lying isn't what friends do? I want more than that with you."

Oh, my god. My brain blanked for a minute, static filling it as I stared at him.

"But I know that's not where we're at," he continued, hopefully unaware of my internal state. "How about you come out to the lodge for dinner again?"

My throat felt thick, and I swallowed. I squeaked again. "Dinner at the lodge?"

He nodded. "Yeah. Daphne's cooking is always good, and it never gets boring."

"Daphne knows about our kiss," I blurted out because blurting things out was my thing today.

He smiled ruefully. "I know, but I didn't tell her. Nora saw us. Nora doesn't care, and

Daphne's the least judgmental person in the universe. No one cares. They won't tease you. If they tease anybody, it'll be me, but it won't be in front of you. I promise. But if that's too much, let me take you out to dinner somewhere else."

I narrowed my eyes. "Like a date?"

He regarded me quietly before nodding slowly. "Yes."

"Do you date?" I couldn't forget what Daphne told me about him.

He eyed me cautiously before replying, "Not usually. But with you, yes."

"Tucker," I warned.

"Skylar," he countered. "I like you. And don't lie to me and tell me there's nothing between us. Let's try this."

I felt crazy. Just bonkers. But my head was stupid and bobbed up and down all on its own. "It's just dinner," I said quickly.

He smiled slightly. "I know. Where do you want to go?"

I didn't have the nerve to tell him that the only restaurants I had tried were the two coffee places Cammi owned and the pizza place. Even though I actually made decent money now, I was constantly waiting for a disaster to happen, so I saved most of it.

As if he could read my mind, he added, "Dinner's on me because I asked you."

I opened my mouth to argue, and he shook his head. "If you ask me out, you can pay."

Pressing my lips together, I took a deep breath before I said, "Fine. Honestly, I don't know where to go. I haven't tried many places."

"What kind of food do you like?" he asked.

"Most everything."

"Well, let's do the brewery. Sally's is good, but it's basically pub food and more of a bar scene. Do you want a busy place like that?"

I shook my head quickly. I hated the bar scene. It was too crowded and too loud and set my nerves on edge.

"All right, the brewery it is. When?"

"I don't know. You're the one asking," I returned, feeling peevish and uncomfortable.

"I know, but I don't know your schedule. I usually have Saturdays off from flying."

"Well, then we should go the day before you have off," I heard myself saying.

"What about your schedule?" he countered patiently.

"I work Sunday through Thursday."

Tucker smiled slowly. "That's perfect. Friday. I'm sure I'll see you before then. Are you coming out to the lodge for yoga on Wednesday?"

I started to shake my head, but he continued, "Come on out. You know Daphne wants you there. Gemma would love to see you."

My heart felt like it might burst. Because I wanted to go. I really did. "Okay, I'll see you there."

He smiled again, letting his hands drop. He startled me when he caught one of my hands in his and reeled me closer. I came to a stumbling stop, maybe six inches in front of him. I swear to God, the man had a presence, and it was *potent*. I could feel his strength, leashed and vibrating.

He held my gaze for several beats before leaning over and brushing a quick kiss across my lips. It felt as if electricity passed between us, shimmering in the air as he drew away. "Have a good evening, Skylar."

He waited while I climbed in my car, fumbling with my keys and trying to scramble my composure together. I took another deep breath before managing to drive away. When I turned down the road that led to the harbor and the gallery with my apartment above it, I wondered if I'd lost my mind.

Chapter Eighteen

TUCKER

"Lift your hands and bring them together over your head," Gemma said in her soothing yoga voice.

I was trying to stay soothed, but Skylar was here this evening. I discovered it wasn't the best plan to have her come to yoga class because I was seriously distracted.

I'd almost been late and ended up a row behind Skylar in the room. Not only did I have an excellent view of the sweet curve of her bottom every time she bent over but I could also see her silhouette from the side. I could see just a hint of her breasts, which were absolutely perfect. I knew that because they filled my palm just so.

Gemma was moving around the class quietly. She paused beside me, using her index finger to adjust my arms, murmuring, "Focus, Tucker."

I risked a glance at her face and saw the sly glint in her eyes. She didn't laugh, though. Gemma rarely lost her composure. I snapped my gaze forward to the mirrors. After Gemma had started running these classes last year, Nora had mirrors installed on one wall. Sometimes we faced the view out the windows and sometimes the mirrors. Unfortunately, when I looked in the mirror, my eyes immediately wandered to glance at Skylar.

Jesus. This was not me. I was not the guy who got distracted by some woman in yoga class. This was supposed to be relaxing. I forced my eyes away and refused, by act of will alone, to look at her again. It was for my own sanity, so I didn't embarrass myself and end up with a hard-on in yoga class.

Once we were done, I bolted out of class, practically running out of the lodge and through the trees to the staff house. I took a cold shower to get through the rest of the night without losing my mind. Doubts skittered along the edge of my thoughts, but the thing was, I wanted Skylar. It felt as if a crack had formed along the side of my heart. The very heart I'd thought was immune to anyone reaching through my guard again.

When I walked through the side entrance at the lodge. I almost collided with Flynn when he was coming out of the door to the private apartment he shared with Daphne. Cat was in the process of moving into the staff house.

"Hey, man," Flynn said as he held open the door to the kitchen for me. "How were your flights today?"

The door swung shut behind me as we walked through. "Uneventful," I replied.

"That's how we like it," he returned. "Should I grab you a beer?" He paused by the opening into the pantry.

"Sure."

"Just grab a six-pack," Grant called.

"Will do," Flynn returned as he cornered into the pantry.

My gaze arced about the kitchen. A few guests were scooping up to-go dinners, which Daphne had started providing on staff-only dinner nights. Many guests went into town for dinner as well.

Skylar was seated at the dining room table, the long table that ran the length of the room in front of the windows. Her dark hair was pulled back in a ponytail, swinging as she turned to reply to something Cammi said.

Diego caught my eyes, winking as he grinned. "You should just go over there," he teased.

"I usually do," I retorted.

Jesus. I didn't even want my friends to know I'd asked Skylar out to dinner. That nugget of information would lead to all kinds of teasing. I loved working with my friends, the friends I considered part of my family, but there were downsides to everybody knowing your business. I didn't think Skylar would say a word about it. She was way too guarded for that.

Flynn appeared at my side again, holding a six-pack in his hand. He handed me a beer from the local brewery.

"What's for dinner?" I asked Daphne as I paused by the corner of the island.

Daphne narrowed her eyes at me. "Just go sit down."

"I don't get to ask what's for dinner? You know I'll love it."

Daphne smiled. "Spicy stir-fry tonight."

"Ooh, that sounds good."

"There are appetizers over on the table," she added.

"Excellent." I cracked open my beer,

tossing the cap in the trash tucked under the counter before striding across the kitchen into the dining area.

I sat down beside Elias, which happened to be across from Skylar, but it was the natural place to sit given the current configuration of people at the table. Cammi was at the end with Elias on the corner beside her and Skylar on her other side. I didn't intend to have a direct line of sight, but now I did.

"How's it going?" I asked Cammi when she cast a smile my way.

"Good."

"You always say good. Is it really always good?" I teased lightly.

She rolled her eyes. "Okay, no. Nobody's life is always good, but it's pretty good. I'm busy, my businesses are running well, and—"

Elias slid an arm around her shoulders, and Cammi's cheeks pinkened. "We're good," she added.

"Remind me when the twins are due?" I asked.

"In four months," Cammi replied, her eyes widening a little as if she hadn't calculated how soon that was.

"Dude, you don't even know what to do with yourself anymore," I teased when Elias leaned down to press a lingering kiss on her cheek.

"What do you mean?" he returned as he lifted his head.

I took a swallow from my beer and grinned. "You're not too cranky anymore."

"He is every morning until he has coffee," Cammi chimed in.

"And he has the best coffee in town at home," I offered as I leaned forward, resting an elbow on the table.

"That must be nice, but you go in early," Skylar commented.

Elias shrugged. "I'm an early riser, no matter what. Cammi leaves before me, but she does make me my own coffee."

"Sometimes, he comes in with me when I'm going to the truck," Cammi piped up.

"Really?" Skylar smiled at them.

Cammi nodded. "He helps me open up."

"Oh, that's sweet," Skylar replied.

Elias narrowed his eyes at Skylar in a mock glare. "Don't call me sweet."

"That *is* sweet," she insisted.

When Skylar's eyes bounced to mine, her cheeks flushed slightly, and then she looked down, reaching for what looked like a fresh spring roll from a tray on the table.

"Those are delicious," Cammi said. "Make sure to use the dipping sauce."

"Does Daphne ever run out of things to make?" Skylar asked after a bite.

"Sometimes she repeats things, but every week there's something new," I replied. "We have our favorites like her chipotle bacon mac and cheese."

"Oh, my fucking god." Elias groaned and turned in his chair, calling to Daphne, "Can you make that next week?"

"Make what?" she called in return.

"Your mac and cheese. We haven't had it on staff night in a while."

"Well, if you still lived here, you'd get it," she retorted.

"I'm not moving back, but I miss that mac and cheese."

Daphne smiled indulgently. "I'll make it next week. Skylar, make sure to come out again."

"Do you like mac and cheese?" Cammi asked her.

Skylar's ponytail bounced with her nod. "I love mac and cheese, but I've only had it out of the box. It's comfort food."

"Oh yeah, straight out of the box is the best comfort food," Cammi agreed.

"Have you ever had it with ketchup?" Elias asked.

Skylar looked at him askance, and he shrugged sheepishly. "Maybe I'm skeptical about that," she replied.

"It's good. It sounds trashy, but it is good. It makes it a little sweeter and a little tangier, I swear," he explained.

"You've never made that for us," Cammi said, looking at him.

"Well, most people are kind of snooty about mac and cheese," Elias said defensively.

"I'm not," Daphne said as she crossed over. "That is a Southern specialty."

"Mac and cheese out of the box with ketchup?" I prompted.

"For sure. Don't bash it until you try it," she countered with a grin.

Chapter Nineteen

SKYLAR

I was silently mortified. There we were, talking about mac and cheese out of the box with ketchup. That was the equivalent of a gourmet meal for me. When I was a kid, condiments could make something crappy taste better. Not that mac and cheese out of the box was crappy.

The meals Daphne made were out of this world for me. I didn't even know how she did it.

"This is amazing," I said between bites once we were eating.

Daphne smiled over at me. "Thank you. Cat did most of the work tonight."

"Thank you," I offered to Cat.

She cast me a quick smile. "Everything I

know in the kitchen Daphne taught me, except the basics."

Nora chimed in, "None of us are that great at cooking."

"At least I'm not alone in that," I said lightly.

"None of us can meet Daphne's standards except for Cat now," Elias said with a grin. "We're all just grateful."

"I'm surprised you moved out and don't come for dinner every night," I said.

"It's a drive and—" He cast a quick glance at Cammi, the look in his eyes intense and intimate. "I had my reasons for moving, and they were worth it."

Cammi blushed slightly before leaning over and pressing a kiss on his cheek. "I'm grateful I'm worth more than Daphne's food, but I understand," she teased.

"It's close," Elias teased in return before taking a bite when she nudged him with her elbow.

I couldn't help but experience a pang of envy. This was a kind of envy where I wished I had that. Somehow maybe someday I would. Of course, that brought to mind that I'd said yes to having dinner with Tucker. That was only two days away with tonight being Wednesday. I wasn't counting. Okay, maybe I was. I'd been worrying over it ever since I'd said yes.

Between stressing about that and trying to forget the kiss and the *way* more than a kiss, I had too many things to think about when it came to Tucker. My thoughts bounced against each other, jostling my anxiety. I recalled the thing Jolene had on her desk. It held a row of hanging silver balls. They would bounce against each other quietly. That was how my thoughts felt when it came to Tucker. They repeated themselves, bouncing from one to the next, leaving me unsettled, flustered, worried, anxious, and so many things. *All* the things.

"Have you seen Risa recently?" Cammi's voice reached me.

I glanced her way. "I run into her here and there. Our schedules don't align, except when she has evening events at the gallery."

"Have you been to any of those?" Daphne prompted.

I shook my head quickly.

"You should go. She has hors d'oeuvres and drinks. It's nice," Cammi added.

"Doesn't it cost money to go?" I asked. I was forever counting pennies and dollars. The lifelong habit of avoiding anything that cost money was deeply ingrained in me.

Daphne and Cammi replied simultaneously, "No."

Cammi looked puzzled, and I felt foolish.
"Oh, I assumed it would."

"The event is free, but the goal is for her
to sell artwork to everyone who's enjoying
their free food and drinks," Cammi said matter-of-factly. "Go if you can. She has them
once a week. Sometimes, she does it over at
Misty Mountain Café, and we do an extra art
display. All of the art on the walls there is for
sale."

"It is?"

Cammi nodded as she smiled. "Yep. Tell
you what. Let's meet at the gallery. Not this
week, but next week."

"We could have girls' night after," Daphne
interjected. "We'll all come down. It's not the
same night as yoga, right?" She looked over
toward Gemma, who shook her head.

"Those gallery events are late enough that
you could come over too," Daphne added.

"Absolutely, I don't offer late yoga classes,"
Gemma replied. "I'd love to do that."

I was surrounded by women who ran
their own businesses—Gemma with her yoga
studio, Cammi with her two businesses, and
everyone at the lodge here. It made me
wonder about my conversation with Ludie. I

really needed to scramble up the nerve to talk to Susie.

"Well?" Cammi prompted.

"I'd love to go. Seeing as I live above the gallery, it's easy," I replied.

"You can meet us downstairs as soon as the art night starts," Daphne offered.

"What exactly happens at art nights?" I asked.

"People walk around and look at the art, and it's an excuse for them to drink, eat, and gossip," Daphne said with a grin.

"Do the guys go?" Cat asked.

"No," Flynn and Elias said while Grant shook his head.

"I've never been," Tucker offered.

"The guys could go, but that would kind of ruin the girls' night thing," Cammi said.

"What if we want to go?" Diego teased.

Gemma nudged him with her elbow. "You can't."

"I feel left out," Grant said.

"Can I come?" Cat asked.

"Of course, but you can't drink," Daphne replied.

"I'll be the designated driver," Cat offered.

"Freaking perfect," Gemma announced. "You can drive all of us."

"I won't need a ride because I live up-stairs," I said.

Just then, I felt Tucker's eyes on me and glanced over. Heat was banked in his gaze, and it felt as if electricity crackled in the air across the table. I looked down at my lap and wondered.

Chapter Twenty

SKYLAR

I stared at myself in the mirror, reaching for my hairbrush again. I ran it through my hair, wrinkling my nose and wishing Emily was here. She often did my hair when we lived in foster care together and later as roommates.

Before I'd sworn off dating, which was a full year before she died, she would do my hair. My hair was stick straight and dark brown. She'd always managed to give it a glossy, tousled look, which I could never pull off. I sighed as I studied my reflection.

"Maybe I need to put it up?" I murmured. "Forget it."

I was having entire conversations with my reflection in the mirror. I reached for some eyeliner. It was smoky gray with a little glitter in it. I felt foolish, but I put it on anyway.

This was ridiculous. I should've canceled. But every time I thought about canceling, I recalled Daphne telling me she had a feeling about Tucker and me. My silly, foolish, battered, and tired heart thumped several beats of hope. Those beats were like claps as if I was cheering myself on.

I told myself Tucker was a nice guy. And maybe, maybe something could happen. At least I told him my story.

After brushing my hair again, I walked out of the bathroom, immediately circling into my bedroom. My apartment was tiny, but it was all mine. Emily and I would've shared the bedroom if she'd been here with me. We'd found a one-bedroom place because we needed to save money. We were cheap, always wanting to save up. The apartment was furnished, so Emily had said it would be a plus. I was enjoying it all by myself even though it was lonely.

I looked at myself in the full-length mirror mounted on the closet door. I was wearing jeans and a pair of boots paired with a fluffy V-neck sweater. At the last minute, I put on a pair of silver hoop earrings.

I didn't usually do things like that. Before

I could change my mind, there was a knock on the door. My heartbeat shot off, rocketing out of control. I tried to take a deep breath, but it was pointless. I could hardly get any air in.

"Get a grip, get a grip, get a grip," I muttered to myself before walking briskly out of the bathroom.

When I opened the door, the force of my motion almost slammed it against the wall. Tucker's reflexes were lightning fast, and he caught the edge of the door on the inside of the hinge.

"Thank you. I guess I kind of overdid it there."

He grinned. His eyes lingered on my face for a minute before skating over me. I felt a flush bloom from the center outward and hoped my cheeks weren't too pink. "Hi," I added belatedly.

"Hey," he said, his voice raspy. "You ready?"

"Sure," I chirped, hurrying to grab my purse off the corner of the kitchen island and slipping into my jacket. He waited for me, and we walked out in silence a few moments later.

I was tense. I tried to remember the last time I went on a date. I still wasn't sure if this *was* a date even though Tucker said it was. I was thinking maybe it was a pity date after everything I'd said to him the other night. Talk about bad habits. I used to do that a lot—tell guys my whole life story—because I was so ready to fall in love. I'd searched for it around every corner. I'd hook up with a guy and think they were looking for love when we'd met at a dive bar. It was ridiculous.

When we got outside, I stopped by my car. His truck was parked right beside it. I looked from him to his truck to my car. "Should I drive?" I finally asked.

"Nooo," he said slowly. "I guess if you really want to drive, you could."

I was relieved for the chilly air because hopefully, it would cool the heat flashing into my cheeks. "I don't need to drive," I finally said.

He actually held the passenger door of his truck open for me, which was weird. Maybe I couldn't remember my last date, but I'd never had a single guy hold the door for me. Not that I thought it was all that important. I was all on board with women, power, and feminism. If someone wanted to hold the door for me, that was polite. Like I held the door for Ludie whenever we walked out together. One time, I gave her a ride home, and I opened the door for her on the passenger side. Maybe I had done it because I needed to clean a few things off the seat, but you get my point.

I didn't date polite guys before. I suppose that was my point.

Once we were seated in his truck, I snuck a glance at Tucker, relieved he wasn't looking at me. He was tapping something on his dashboard. "Hot or cold?" he asked.

"What do you mean?"

"I have dual controls and heated seats."

"I'm usually cold," I replied.

"Does seventy-four sound good?"

Seventy-four seemed downright decadent. Another holdover from growing up poor was no matter what the temperature was in the winter, the heat never went above sixty-five. That was warm enough to keep you from getting hypothermia, but when it was really cold and rainy out, I wouldn't have minded being a little warmer.

Once he started driving, his hand rested casually on the steering wheel. His fingers dangled over the edge, and his forearm was dusted lightly with brown-gold hair. I soaked up the little details about him.

A short drive later, our footsteps

crunched on the gravel as we crossed the parking lot to Diamond Creek Brewery. It wasn't far from the airport. I'd always been curious, yet I'd never dared to go. Financially, I was fine. Frankly, I was better than I'd ever been. Yet the habits of constantly squirreling away what little money I had and worrying about it all falling apart were grooved so deep in my brain, sometimes it felt as if I'd tripped and fallen into them.

A little hum of anticipation buzzed through me. It wasn't even about Tucker. I was going out to dinner at a new restaurant, and that was a big deal for me. The restaurant was in an old airplane hangar, completely renovated. The outside looked mostly the same, except windows had been cut into the corrugated steel walls. It was situated beside a marshy field, just beyond a narrow stream that fed the ocean from Kachemak Bay. A sign in a whimsical font was mounted above the entrance.

Tucker held the door for me, and I scooted in, surprised to discover the waiting area was crowded with people. "I made a reservation," he murmured, his voice just beside my ear and sending a shiver down that side of my body.

When his hand landed on the curve of my

back, his touch was like a hot shock. The heat of it filtered through my clothing. He coaxed me forward when I came to a stop. "Excuse us," he murmured.

His voice was low but authoritative, and the crowd parted for us. "Shouldn't we wait?" I asked under my breath.

"Nope. That's what reservations are for."

Seconds later, we were standing in front of a small reception stand, and a woman dressed in jeans and combat boots with a pretty silky blouse smiled at us. Her dark blond hair was pulled into a ponytail that swung as she moved. "Hey, Tucker."

"Hey, Lana," he said easily. "We have a reservation."

She glanced down at a notepad sitting on the stand in front of her. "That you do, Tucker Harrison." She picked up two menus. "Follow me."

I was totally blown away by this. We just skipped the whole line. It felt insane. I'd never made a reservation anywhere in my entire life. Emily and I had dreams when we were young about making reservations at one of the fanciest restaurants in San Francisco. But it was too expensive and too exclusive, something we never had the nerve to do. That was a depressing thing about poverty and uncertainty. Even dreaming big felt like asking for too much. Reservations at a restaurant weren't too big for Tucker, though.

A moment later, Lana stopped in front of a table by the windows in the corner. This also felt as if we were breaking some kind of rule. This wasn't supposed to be our table. It had the best view in the entire restaurant and privacy to boot.

"Here you are," Lana said with an easy smile cast between us. "Have a seat. Do you want to know the specials?" She set the menus down in front of each chair before holding up a smaller one, offering, "These are the specials. The king crab is heavenly."

"Whew. I love king crab," Tucker commented.

"Would you like some drinks?" she asked.

Tucker glanced at me, and I shrugged. "I don't know."

"Well, Danny will be your server. He'll be here in just a few minutes. You can let him know. The drink menu is right there." She gestured to a small laminated menu tucked between the salt and pepper.

"Okay, thank you," Tucker said.

After we sat down, she hurried off. Tucker lifted his gaze to mine. "Get whatever you want."

"We're splitting the check, right?"

He narrowed his eyes, shaking his head. "No."

"Yes, we are," I insisted. "Remember? You got the pizza the other night."

"But I asked you out to dinner," he replied as if that settled it.

I opened my mouth to argue, startled when he shrugged. "You know what? Whatever. If you want to split the check, we can."

My expression must have given away my surprise because he flashed a grin, his sky-blue eyes crinkling at the corners. "Surprised you, didn't I?"

"Yeah," I muttered. "Maybe I will have you pay."

"That's fine too."

I rolled my eyes. "Are you getting something to drink?" I asked.

He shook his head. "I'm driving. I could have a beer, but it's easier not to worry about it."

"Then I won't have anything."

"But you're not driving."

"I know, but I don't drink much anyway." I opened the menu, asking, "What are you getting?"

He didn't even open the menu. "Oh, I'm getting that king crab special."

"I've never had king crab."

His mouth dropped open. "What?!"

"It's crazy expensive."

"You need to try it," he insisted.

"But we can't get the same thing."

"Let's get the king crab appetizer, and then you get something else. We can share."

Anxiety tightened in my chest. Navigating the treacherous waters of ordering in a restaurant felt overwhelming. I knew what to get at a fast food place—double cheeseburger, extra pickles. That was my favorite.

Tucker was waiting, his eyes on me. I took a breath before opening the menu and staring down at it, relieved to see the choices weren't too overwhelming.

"Have you been here before?" I asked.

"Oh, yeah. We come here pretty regularly."

"Who's we?"

"Anyone from the lodge. Good food, good pizza. Honestly, everything's good." He leaned over, pointing at something on the menu. "That's good."

"Halibut tacos?" I asked doubtfully.

"I promise. They're good," he assured me.

"Okay, I'll get them."

That got me another grin, and butterflies

swarmed in my belly. My lungs felt tight as I tried to suck in a breath of air.

Just then, a young man paused by our table. "Hi there."

"Hey, Danny," Tucker said with an easy grin and a wink. "Have you met Skylar?"

Danny shook his head as he smiled down at me. He was handsome with dark blond hair, brown eyes, and a relaxed manner. "Can't say I've had the pleasure. Danny Turner at your service."

"Skylar, Skylar Bridges," I replied with a smile.

"Have you two decided what you'd like tonight? Anything to drink?"

"I'll take a bottle of your non-alcoholic cider," Tucker said.

"Oh, I'll take the same," I chimed in.

"Perfect, that stuff is good," Danny said.

"We're ready to order too," Tucker added.

"I'll take the halibut tacos," I said when Tucker looked at me.

He ordered his king crab and a hot pretzel stuffed with more crab. On the docks in San Francisco were cheap fish markets with good prices and the like, so I'd had crab, but I'd never had the vaunted king crab.

Danny disappeared, and we fell quiet before Tucker commented, "I can't believe you haven't been here before. Tell me what else you haven't tried since you've been to Alaska."

"I don't really do restaurants," I said, deciding honesty was my best approach.

His brows hitched up. "No?"

"They're expensive. I'm not used to having much spending money. It's a habit." I shrugged, trying to ignore the self-consciousness welling inside.

"I know Ludie pays you well. That's a good job."

"I know. Like I said, it's a habit. You're a pilot, so I'm guessing you make more money than me."

He winked. "I am, but it's not about the money. You at least need to try all the good places in Diamond Creek. That doesn't even cover Anchorage, where there are plenty of good restaurants."

"Anchorage is over four hours away," I squeaked.

"Yeah, it's a day trip," he replied with a shrug.

I let out a startled laugh.

"It's Alaska. I thought it was weird how people barely paid attention to geographic distance when I first moved here too, but now it's not. It's just the way it is."

"I know," I agreed. "People fly to Anchorage for the day. Do you guys do many of those flights?"

"Here and there."

Tucker was good at social conversation, or so I discovered that night. This was a side of him I hadn't seen, and I had no idea what to think of it. At the lodge with his friends, I'd seen his relaxed side. But this was even more different. It felt like he was actually trying to make an effort, and I sensed he was trying to put me at ease. *That* unsettled me because I wasn't supposed to matter. Not to anyone.

Chapter Twenty-One

TUCKER

Skylar was nervous, and I found myself trying to put her at ease. I was a good friend, but my friends were easy. They all knew me well. We'd formed an unbreakable bond in our time in the Air Force together. We'd been living and working together for years. The weave of those bonds only strengthened. They knew I liked to keep to myself and didn't mind it.

When I was younger, I was more social. But life could mete out harsh lessons some-times. When Claire died, I lost touch with my easygoing side. I kept to myself. It was easier that way. Although I'd told myself for years that I didn't want to let anyone matter too much, I knew my friends mattered as much as Claire did. But those relationships were different.

Falling in love required strength. I simply didn't know if I had it in me anymore. So when it came to women, I didn't really try, not much at all. And maybe I was an asshole because of that.

Skylar sat across from me, worrying about saving money instead of eating out at a restaurant. Maybe I didn't understand that lesson in life. I'd had a stable childhood with two parents who took care of me. They had always been there for me.

I wanted Skylar to have that certainty. I wanted her to stop worrying, to believe life could be okay. This whole thing was fucking crazy. I wasn't *that* guy—protective and taking care of other people. Oh, I had been with Claire. I'd been *so* in love with her. Even now, I tried to look back and tell myself it was just because I was young. I had been young, and there was something to that kind of love—an innocence to it, a headlong, rushed quality that I doubted could be repli- cated, but it ran deep, and it cut even deeper. When she got sick and fucking died, I learned just how brutally unfair life could be. The old muscle memory was there, though. I knew how to make an effort.

I sensed Skylar was even skeptical about my effort, which made me silently laugh a little. Perhaps, I'd finally encountered someone more guarded than me, which was saying something.

She loved the king crab. After two bites, she looked up at me. "Oh, my god," she moaned.

"I told you it was good."

She actually smiled. "Wow. It's amazing."

"Don't get king crab anywhere other than Alaska, though."

"No?"

"It's pricey here, but it's obscene everywhere else because they have to fly it out, so..."

"It's even more expensive," Skylar finished my sentence for me, her eyes widening slightly. "It's so good, though."

"I know."

She flashed a rare smile then, and I felt like I'd won something, a tiny something, but something nevertheless. There I was, trying to put Skylar at ease and wrestling with my body's reaction to her.

Fuck me. She was so delectably cute. She had this tomboyish quality with a femininity underneath that I sensed she tried to hide, though she didn't hide it well. With her dark hair gleaming under the lights and her big blue eyes, she was stunning. Her skin was soft and silky, and I knew how it felt to have her come all over my fingers. Before I'd gone to pick her up tonight, I told myself this was just dinner, but my body had a different opinion.

My body thought we should have dinner, and I should take her back to her place and not leave until I was buried deep inside her. Even then, that might not be enough to slake the need rampaging through me.

Danny brought our check. I slipped my credit card out and glanced at Skylar. "Well?"

"What?" she asked.

"Are we splitting the check or not?"

She eyed me for a few beats before pulling her wallet out. "We're splitting."

I shrugged. "Okay, or I have another idea."

"What?" She eyed me skeptically, a little wrinkle forming between her brows.

"I cover tonight, and then you get the next place."

Pink washed over her cheeks in a rush. "What?"

"Have you had dinner at the lodge?"

"Um, last week?"

"I meant the ski lodge."

She bit her lip before replying. "No. I've heard about it."

"That's our next dinner date."

She twisted her lips to the side, eyeing me carefully. "I don't know."

"You don't know what? If you want to eat at the ski lodge, or if you want to have dinner with me."

Skylar let out a sigh. "Both."

I didn't want to admit how much that bothered me, but I wasn't going to let it show. "You can think about it. The offer stands."

"What do you mean the offer stands?"

"Just generally speaking. There's no deadline on it."

"What do you mean?"

"Exactly that."

"But..."

"If you decide you want to go, you can let me know." I wanted to push a little, just a little, but Skylar was seriously skittish.

She pulled the check across the table and literally tapped her finger on each row. A few seconds later, she announced the split. Danny returned and took my credit card and her cash.

Chapter Twenty-Two

TUCKER

Skylar glanced toward the sunset over the marsh when we stepped out into the parking area. It was a stunner. Although Alaska spoiled you like that. Every day was a stunner. An eagle screeched, and Skylar glanced around.

"What is that?" she asked.

I paused, looking down at her. "It's an eagle."

"That's an eagle?" Her eyes widened. "It's all screechy."

Just then, the eagle in question screeched again as it lifted off from a tree along the edge of the marsh. We started walking again. Without thinking, I reached for her hand. "This way."

"Where?" she asked. She stiffened slightly, but then her hand relaxed in mine.

I pointed with my other hand toward the walkway off to one side of the parking lot. It was just beyond where I'd parked.

"Oh!" Her eyes lit up.

She walked with me onto the wooden walkway that led out over the marsh. She dropped my hand, curling both of hers on the railing. Leaning against it, she looked out, her gaze scanning the horizon. "It's so beautiful," she breathed.

"It is. I've been here over four years, and I honestly haven't gotten used to it yet."

She looked up at me. "No?"

I shook my head and pointed toward a cluster of alder trees to one side of this marshy area. "There are a few moose over there."

Her head whipped around. "Oh! They're so big. Ludie tells me to be careful around moose."

"Yeah, they're nearsighted. By the time you're close enough for them to see you, they can charge you pretty quick. More people get hurt by moose than bears."

"I don't want to see a grizzly or a brown bear," she announced firmly. "What's the difference anyway?"

"I've been told brown bears are along the coast. So, any you see around here would be browns. Grizzlies are in the interior, away from the coastline. Grizzlies are a little smaller than brown bears."

"Why is that?" she prompted.

"Because they have a kick-ass diet on the coast, all that salmon."

"Seriously?"

I shrugged. "Makes sense. I'm with you on seeing them, though. I don't need to see a brown bear or grizzly bear up close. I see them here and there when I'm flying."

"You do?"

"Oh, yeah. Have you been across the bay in a plane?"

Skylar's hair swung as she shook her head. "Well, that does it. I'm taking you for a ride."

"You don't need to do that."

"You can ride along when I have a delivery trip."

I would've offered to take her on a tour, but I knew Skylar wouldn't agree to that. She turned to look out over the marshy field, her eyes scanning the sky, which was outdoing itself this evening with shades of pink, lavender, and hints of a bloodred staining the sky. I could appreciate the view, but I was more focused on wanting to kiss Skylar. Something fierce.

We fell quiet. Alaska never failed to remind me of one shining thing. You could forget yourself if you just fell into the moment. The beauty was stark, so encompassing. While my need to kiss Skylar didn't abate, it twined within the quiet of the twilight. The light thinned into darkness. Second by second, the stars were starting to show. The soft gust of a salty breeze came from the bay across the marsh.

Skylar made a sound, something like a sigh. I glanced down just as she peered up at me. Her cheeks were tinged pink from the cool spring air. Because I wasn't thinking, my need led me. Angling to face her, I waited a moment before I dipped down, giving her time to turn away, to tell me another kiss was stupid, but she didn't.

I couldn't say for certain, but I thought she leaned up to meet me as I bent low. Her lips were warm. A shock of electricity sizzled between us when I fit my mouth over hers. She let out a soft sigh into our kiss, and then our tongues were tangling, and the kiss went on and on and on. It got hot and deep *fast*.

I lost sense of where we were until the sound of a raven calling nearby, loud and sharp in the twilight sky, snapped through the haze of my need and punctured my awareness. We broke apart, our breath ragged in the quiet air.

Skylar was pressed against me. I had one arm banded around her waist and the other cupping her nape. I trailed my thumb across the side of her neck and over the wild thrum of her pulse. I stepped back, reflexively reaching for her hand. Just as my fingers laced with hers, I expected her to tug away, but she didn't.

Chapter Twenty-Three

SKYLAR

For every second of the short drive from the restaurant back to my apartment, my body shimmered with energy. Like those nights when there was nothing but nature to be heard—the call of an owl, the rustle of leaves in the wind, insects chirping, and the sound of waves breaking on the shore. That was how my body felt. All of my senses were attuned and alive, shifting and twitching, everything heightened to Tucker.

Maybe I didn't understand what he saw in me, but I knew he wanted me despite all of the muddled confusion I carried about relationships and trust. I understood desire and lust. I recognized the bell clanging and my body vibrating in response and knew I wasn't alone in my need and desire.

The rush of it tuned out the critical voices in my head, which was no easy feat. The only reason I was able to manage it was because I was too needy, and it swamped me. I could feel the damp silk between my thighs. My nipples were tight, and my skin felt prickly, chafing for Tucker's touch.

I knew I was going to invite him in. I also knew I might regret it later, but I didn't care. Not right then. Rational thought and reason were washed away in the riptide of lust.

The sound of his blinker echoed loudly when he turned into the parking area at the gallery. When his eyes slipped to mine, without a word, I knew he was asking if he should park in the front or the back. I nodded, nudging my chin toward the back, silently answering, *"Yes, I want you. Yes, we're doing this."*

The sound of the gravel under his tires rumbled through my system, spinning into the vibration of sensations. His engine went quiet a moment later, followed by that subtle clicking sound. As the engine cooled, my body revved.

"Should I walk you up?" Tucker asked.

With every ounce of boldness I could

muster, I turned to face him and answered, "I want you to come in."

He stared at me in the dim light cast from the parking lot lighting. His eyes searched mine for a few beats before he dipped his chin in acknowledgment.

We rushed up the stairs, our footsteps echoing in the hallway above the gallery. With mine the only apartment, the space felt alone, almost as if we weren't supposed to be here. The studio was dark, and the gallery was closed downstairs.

We reached my door, and I fumbled for my keys.

"Skylar," Tucker said.

My eyes swung to his, and then he was kissing me, pressing me against the wall beside the door.

Oh. My. God. His kisses were sinfully good—a mix of bold and bossy, gentle and assured. Deep sweeps of his tongue, nips on my lips, and then drawing away, punctuating it with a soft kiss on one corner of my mouth. Just one. Butterflies took flight in my belly, sending sensations like little sparks leaping from a fire throughout my body.

I broke free. Breathless, I dragged in a deep gulp of air. His intent blue eyes stared down at mine.

"Are you sure you want me to come in?" he pressed.

"You'd better," I retorted, lifting my chin and narrowing my eyes. I was irrational and insecure and needy when it came to the emotional part of relationships. But I was bold and almost reckless when it came to sex.

A therapist I'd liked had once said that might be part of my neediness. Because I could try to grab on and hope and hope and hope. I let down my barriers, shaking off my emotional fear, letting the lust and need and desire drive me.

I didn't think about any of that now. I knew my recriminations and questions would come later, but not tonight.

I held strong under his gaze. "Okay," he whispered gruffly.

Moments later, after I dropped my keys and he helped me get them into the lock, we were in my apartment. I didn't let anything slow this down. I reached for his hand, reeling him to me. His eyes widened slightly, but that didn't give me pause. Nothing would, not tonight, not now.

This might be the only night I had with him, and I was going to grab it with both hands and enjoy every single second.

"This," I murmured as I arched against him, sliding my hand around his neck.

He met me halfway, his lips fitting over mine. Maybe I was being reckless and bold, but the second his tongue swept into my mouth, he took control of our kiss. He spun me and nudged me backward until I felt my hips bump against the couch.

I almost stumbled, but he caught me, steadying me and lifting me as he sat down on the couch.

"Oh, I like this," I murmured when I broke away to gasp.

Straddling him, I could feel the hard ridge of his arousal. I was already toeing the edge of an orgasm, which should have alarmed me. There *was* a distant alarm ringing in the corner of my mind, but I ignored it.

I shouldn't have been that primed. It shouldn't have felt this easy. Yet it was with Tucker. I lost myself, that riptide pulling me farther and farther out to sea, into this moment—one after the other with him, each one tumbling into the next. It was like water rushing over a cliff.

We tugged at each other's clothes. It was rushed and messy. Scrambling off his lap, I ordered him to yank his shirt off. He did with alacrity, the sound of his gruff chuckle sending shivers over my skin. Moments later, I was bare save for my panties. His jeans were tossed beside mine on the floor. He wore fitted navy-blue boxers, his arousal jutting out. I reached to tug them down, but he caught my hands, murmuring something.

I didn't know what. Before I could even protest, he was kissing me again, spreading me out on the couch. His lips closed over a nipple, and I cried out as sensation arrowed sharply to my core. I clenched all over. His fingers delved, wasting no time to yank my panties down. I kicked them free, letting out a moan of satisfaction followed by a whimper when his fingers teased into my slick folds and sank inside.

I was so ready. My hips bucked up against him. He murmured something against my neck before lifting his head and drawing his fingers out. "Let's slow this down."

"No!" I protested.

Something rose fiercely inside me. It felt almost feral, tangling with emotions I didn't want to contemplate.

He brushed my hair away from my face. He didn't reply with words, but the kisses he dropped on my lips and then on my neck said *easy, easy.*

I wanted to buck against it. I felt like a

wild pony, but somehow, he soothed me. His hands mapped my body. He kindled the fire higher and higher inside while my restless need rose sharply and the bite of unsettled emotions dissolved.

He dusted kisses across my trembling belly, pushing a knee to the side. On the heels of a gasp, his mouth was on my sex, and my hands were gripping his hair. I cried out sharply. I was so close to the edge, my orgasm just waiting. One wave of pleasure rolled into the next, and then his fingers sank inside when he licked deeply into me.

The wave broke, crashing and catching me in it. I shuddered hard, hearing myself let out a keening cry. I pulled his hair so hard I was surprised it didn't hurt.

A moment later, he was rising above me. We hadn't discussed birth control, but apparently, he had more sense than I did because he had produced a condom out of seemingly nowhere. I could only think he must've planned ahead. But then, he was a prepared kind of guy. He smoothed it on swiftly. His gaze bored into mine as his weight came over me.

I should've been surprised. I liked to be in control. But then, it was obvious I wasn't in control.

With Tucker, I didn't suppose I had been in control since before he even kissed me that first time. All of it felt as if I was spinning loose, like flotsam across the surface of the ocean in a storm.

I felt the muscled planes of his chest, the hot shock of his skin against mine. His eyes were almost violet in the dim light in my living room. I felt the nudge of his crown at my entrance, followed by the thick stretch and glide of him filling me. I heard myself whispering, "This."

Chapter Twenty-Four

TUCKER

I kept my eyes on Skylar's, watching as they widened as I felt her silky clench tighten around me until I was sheathed fully inside her. I let out a groan in my throat when I seated myself deeply and nudged once again as if in punctuation.

She whispered, "This," again, and I knew precisely what she meant. This, *all* of this. Her, me, us. Twined together, a shimmering net of passion holding us close.

She stared at me, something like fear flickering in the depths of her wide eyes for a moment. I didn't sense she was afraid of me. There was an emotional quality to it, almost primal. The same emotion I'd picked up on earlier. The recklessness, the dashing, the shying away from any feeling. It was almost as if she was afraid to feel.

At this moment, I didn't have much control. I clung to the thread of it, frayed but not yet snapped. I held still for several beats before dropping my head and kissing her. Her tongue darted out, gliding boldly against mine. Drawing back, I filled her, again and again. Her hips arched to meet every thrust. Her skin was dewy against mine.

My release was already spinning tight. I tried to hang on, to slow down, but she urged me on. One heel dug into the back of a thigh, the other against my hip. She was so wet and so tight, and the sounds she made, oh, my god. Fuck me. Raspy moans and throaty whimpers.

I saw her sassy, bossy side. "Hurry, please. Now," she demanded.

I couldn't do anything other than give her what she asked for because it was exactly what I wanted. I felt her release threatening again when she tightened, clamping around me. She shuddered roughly, crying out and shouting my name.

My own release finally snapped, lightning sizzling from the base of my spine as I surged to fill her once more. A guttural cry followed, and I trembled all over. I fell against her, gulping in air. For a moment, I couldn't even move. Gathering myself, I braced on one elbow so I didn't crush her.

I shifted, rolling over as soon as I could. I was still inside her as she fell against me, sated and soft. I could feel the beat of her heart against my chest as my own thundered along with it.

I had no idea how long we lay there. When my awareness flickered, my fingers were sifting through the ends of her hair. Her palm was flat against my chest. I wanted to stay right there, but that was crazy.

I wondered what she was thinking. Eventually, she lifted her head, and we stared at each other. That fear I'd seen earlier flickered in her eyes but disappeared just as quickly. I wanted to say something, but I knew that was treacherous. This whole moment was treacherous for me, and I sensed it also was for her.

"You have to go home," she announced.

"I do?"

She nodded. I wanted to ask why, but I knew she wouldn't tell me, so I didn't.

"Okay."

A moment later, she was scrambling off my lap and handing me my clothes. I got dressed although not as fast as her. She had her clothes on inside of a minute, or so it seemed.

A weighted few moments later, she was standing by her kitchen counter, eyeing me warily. You'd have never known we'd just been tangled up skin to skin.

"Thank you for dinner," she said politely.

"Of course. Where are we having dinner next?" I asked, knowing I was pushing it.

When she opened her mouth to speak, I was pretty sure she was going to argue the point. Then she closed it and took a breath before replying, "How about the ski lodge?"

I felt like I had won a major victory, but I didn't dare gloat. "Next Friday?"

She nodded. I kissed her before I left, but it was brief. Driving home, I wondered if I had lost my mind. I didn't want to see that look of fear and vulnerability in Skylar's eyes. I wanted to make it go away forever.

But there was a catch. That meant facing my own fear. I thought I knew something she didn't believe. People could be good. You could count on someone. But trying to show her that meant me counting on the universe not to play another cruel joke on me.

My faith was shaky on that point.

Chapter Twenty-Five

SKYLAR

I heard a soft swishing sound, or maybe a slipping sound, followed by a heavy tumble. I had just finished work for the day and spun in my chair to see Ludie on the floor across the hallway.

"Oh, my god!" I exclaimed, leaping up and dashing into her office.

"I'm fine," she murmured, her voice thready.

"Ludie, I think you just fainted." I knelt beside her.

"No, I didn't, sweetie," she said, her voice a little stronger.

"I'm calling 911," I said as I fumbled for my phone in my pocket.

She shook her head. "Call Dan. He's outside helping Flynn and his brother with something," she managed between shaky breaths.

I dialed Dan's number quickly. He answered immediately. "Skylar, Dan here."

"Hey, Dan. Ludie fainted. I wanted to call 911, but she told me to call you." I was already questioning why I'd done as she asked.

"I'm completely conscious, for God's sake," she said, her voice even stronger this time.

"Be right there. Call 911," Dan ordered me.

I knew Ludie could hear him because her eyes narrowed. I sat beside her on the floor, holding the phone to my ear after I dialed 911.

"911, what's your emergency?"

"Hi, I'm out at the small airport, and my boss fainted."

"I didn't faint," she protested beside me.

The 911 operator ran through a few questions before asking how Ludie was now.

"She is conscious and has been since I got into the room, but her skin is pale and—" I held my fingers to the pulse on her wrist. "Her pulse feels thin if that's a thing. I don't know."

"Ma'am, we'll have an emergency vehicle there within five minutes. Will you be able to wait with her?"

"Of course! I'm not going anywhere." As if on cue, I heard the door burst open from out front. "Her husband just got here too. Should I stay on the line?"

"You can if you'd like, or you can call again if you need to. The EMTs are already on the way."

Ludie glared at me. "I'll call back if I need to," I said hurriedly.

As soon as I hung up, Dan entered the room. He knelt in front of Ludie. "What happened?" he asked gruffly.

He stared at Ludie with so much love in his eyes that my heart felt pierced by it. It took my breath away for a few seconds. Not that I'd ever doubted Dan's love for her or hers for him, but they'd been together a long time. They had a shorthand, casual manner with each other that tended toward practical. This moment felt intimate.

"I'm fine," she insisted. "If Skylar wasn't still working, she wouldn't even be over here. She heard me slip. That's all."

"Ludie," Dan said, a hint of warning in his tone.

"All right. I fell. I'm glad she checked on

me, but I swear, I'm okay. I was never un-conscious."

"You have that thing going on with your heart," Dan interjected.

"What's going on with your heart?" I burst in.

"Her heart skips a beat sometimes," he explained. "Sometimes, she gets weak be-cause she doesn't get enough oxygen in her blood."

"Should we be doing something about this?" I practically yelped.

"I take medicine," Ludie said defensively.

I might have only known Ludie and Dan for less than a year, but they were more family than I'd ever had. They treated me like their own, and I cared about them. More than I wanted to admit.

"She takes medicine, but sometimes, she forgets. I'm getting you one of them pillbox-es," Dan announced.

Ludie rolled her eyes, pressing her lips to-gether. I knew she was feeling stronger for that alone. "Pillboxes are for old people."

"Well, Ludie, we are officially old. Nothing wrong with a pillbox," Dan said.

"It's like a calendar. It'll just help you keep organized for the day-to-day. That's all," I offered, trying to ignore the lump in my throat and the way my chest ached.

"Fine, I'll get a pillbox," Ludie muttered, her eyes bouncing between Dan and me. She looked as if we'd betrayed her.

At that moment, we heard voices out front, and I leaped up, hurrying down the hallway to greet the EMT crew. A police officer was with them, and I instantly got nervous. I didn't know why, but if a cop was in the vicinity, I assumed I had done something wrong. I used to joke with Emily that if I came across someone who'd been murdered, even if the murderer was standing there with a knife over the body, I would feel like I had done it just for being present. We both speculated that perhaps that was an unintended side effect of being in foster care. You had so many authority figures coming in and out of your life and making decisions for you that you tended to feel like you were always out of place and being judged.

I thought this man might be Risa's husband, which should have relaxed me, but I was still nervous.

"Ludie okay?" the police officer asked.

"I'm not sure. She fainted," I said over my shoulder as I led the group down the hallway.

All the while, my heart thudded in my chest. I wanted to cry, but I needed to keep my shit together. Dan had shifted from kneeling in front of Ludie to sitting on his hips beside her. They were both resting against the desk. The EMTs went into action.

Ludie swatted them away. "What are you doing here?" she asked, her eyes swinging up to the police officer.

"I happened to be nearby when I heard the call. I wanted to make sure you're okay," the man said easily. He glanced at Dan. "How's it going, Dan?"

"Hey, Darren. Ludie's being stubborn again. She doesn't want a pillbox so she'll remember her heart meds."

Ludie looked horrified. Dan was spilling her personal tea right here. One of the EMTs asked Dan a question, and the cop glanced at me. "I don't think we've met. I'm Darren Thomas, chief of police for Diamond Creek."

"I'm Skylar, Skylar Bridges." My voice felt as small as I felt. "I work here," I added.

"I know," Darren said with a nod.

"Oh, you probably know everything, huh?"

"No, I definitely don't. But you rent from Risa. She mentioned you're a friend. Any friend of hers is a friend of mine," he said easily.

I didn't know what to do with this, so I just nodded. Risa's husband and Diamond Creek's chief of police was one handsome man. With chocolate brown hair and eyes to match, he was relaxed and masculine. After our brief conversation, he was swept into chatting with Ludie and Dan. The EMTs didn't end up taking her to the hospital, but they gave her oxygen on-site and procured a pillbox from their vehicle, donating it to her. She wanted to argue the point until they pointed out she donated funds to the town's emergency services every year.

"We'll just pretend you gave it to yourself," one of them said.

Ludie laughed softly. Her color had come back.

"You might want to think about getting an emergency button," Darren commented.

"What?!" Ludie barked.

"In here, in the bathroom, and at your house," Darren added.

"Why?" she demanded. "I'm fine."

"If Skylar hadn't been here and heard you, you might've needed more help," Dan said pointedly.

Eventually, the emergency crew filtered

out. Darren left with a wave, and I made sure Ludie and Dan were buckled up in Dan's car, insisting I would close up everything. I returned to the office, looking around and thinking about how I'd never been in here without Ludie and Dan.

It was getting dark outside. The office layout was simple. The front entrance faced the parking area with the runway just beyond that. The rows of plane hangars lined it on the other side. In the distance beyond that, Diamond Creek's larger airport, the one where the big planes landed, was visible. There were a few chairs and a desk with some magazines strewn across the top in the front area. No one ever sat at that desk. I walked down the short hallway that led to Ludie's office on one side with the break room across from it. That room had a round table, a microwave, and a small refrigerator. Just past that, at the end of the hallway, was the room where we manned the airwaves to coordinate transports and online scheduling. It held an L-shaped desk with computer monitors and phones.

Ludie and Dan had started this business well before the era of cell phones. They still had the old dial-up phones lined up even though we never used them. I needed to ask Susie about a small business loan. If something happened to Ludie and Dan, I really did want this to be mine.

Oh, I'd be scared as hell, but I loved this job, and I thought I was actually pretty good at it. Having something to focus on kept my mind from spinning off down myriad tracks of anxiety, worry, and regret, and recrimination. They were all there waiting in my thoughts. I took a deep breath, almost jumping out of my skin when I heard the door open out front.

I hurried down there to see Tucker coming in. "Hey, I was coming into land, and I heard from Flynn that Ludie had an emergency. He said Dan called and said she was okay, but I thought I'd see how she was doing."

"She did. She fainted," I said.

"She okay?" he pressed.

I nodded, my eyes stinging with the tears threatening to spill over. "I think so. Apparently, she has some kind of heart condition where her heart skips a beat sometimes. She's supposed to take medicine, and she forgets. I guess she doesn't always get enough oxygen. That's what Dan told me."

I was standing by that desk out front, my fingertips resting on the edge. Tucker's eyes held mine from across the room. "You okay, Skylar?" he asked, his tone gentle.

It actually hurt to swallow, but I tried to put on a brave face. "Yeah, I'm fine," I croaked.

In a second, Tucker was right in front of me, pulling me into his arms. I buried my face in his chest and burst into tears. He smelled like the wind and the trees with a hint of salty ocean air clinging to him. I wasn't the kind of girl who burst into tears. I wasn't the kind of girl who let any man comfort her, even though it was always what I'd been desperate for.

———

I tried to pull myself together, but I couldn't. Every time I lifted my head and tried to look at Tucker, I cried even harder. Everything I attempted to say came out in a garble of hitched breath and sobs. He simply held me, one palm moving in slow passes up and down my back. His touch was so soothing, and it felt beyond good to be in his arms.

He was warm and strong and seemed entirely unruffled by my explosion of tears. I finally reached a point when my crying slowed. By then, I was afraid to even look at him. I was mortified.

My head was tucked against his chest. I heard the rumble of his voice against my cheek when he spoke. "Everybody needs a good cry sometimes."

"I know," I mumbled to his chest. "But I don't cry."

"I do sometimes," he said, his voice low and gravelly.

That punctured my embarrassment. I cautiously lifted my head, peering up at him. I had one arm banded tightly around his waist and the other tucked between us. I knuckled my tears with my fist as a watery, sheepish smile stretched across my face. "Sorry about that."

"It's okay. You worried about Ludie?"

I swallowed and nodded. "Maybe this sounds weird, but Ludie and Dan are like family for me even though I haven't been here that long."

"I get it. There are different kinds of family."

"She scared me today."

He nodded, his palm still soothing me

with those slow passes. "What do you want to do?"

"What do you mean?" I asked, genuinely puzzled.

"Well, I'm not leaving you alone tonight," he said bluntly. "After a cry like that, I'd be a shitty friend to walk away."

"No, you wouldn't." I shrugged, feeling foolish. "It's just me and my drama."

"Do you want to come out to the lodge for dinner?"

I shook my head swiftly at that. I wasn't ready for a crowd even though I liked everyone there.

Blessedly, Tucker didn't ask me to explain. He simply dipped his chin in acknowledgment. "Do you want a distraction?"

"What do you mean?"

"Well, we could get takeout and go back to your place, or I could take you out somewhere."

I wasn't ready to see people who knew me that well, but a distraction might help me pull myself together. It was enough for Tucker to have seen me fall apart. I could handle strangers. "Okay," I said quietly.

"Ski lodge, or go somewhere else?"

"Let's go to the ski lodge. I heard it's really good."

"Oh, it's good. Trust me. Come on."

He loosened his hold, his hands sliding down my arms as he stepped back. He curled his palm around one of mine, and I savored the feel of it. I needed the contact to ground me, to keep me from feeling like I was spinning loose. Feeling lost and unmoored was common when you spent so much time alone.

When we walked outside, I came to a stumbling stop as I looked at the sky. It was painted in streaks of red, pink, and orange, with the last rays of the sun shooting through the colors. I pressed my palm against my chest as I took a breath.

"Kind of like living in a postcard here," Tucker commented.

Smiling up at him, I felt a little lighter inside. "It does."

I heard the screech of an eagle and a few seagulls calling nearby. I breathed in the crisp salty air. Our footsteps crunched on the gravel as we walked through the parking area. I discovered Tucker was parked beside my car.

"I'll follow you back to your place, so you can drop your car off," he said. I opened my mouth to argue, and he added, "For the environment. It's about a twenty-minute drive up the hill. It seems silly for both of us to drive up and back."

"Well, when you say it like that, all logical and stuff, it makes sense," I said dryly.

He squeezed my hand before he let it go.

Chapter Twenty-Six

TUCKER

"Oh, my god," Skylar moaned after she finished chewing. "This is so good."

She'd ordered salmon with some kind of lemon mustard glaze, and I'd ordered seared halibut. "I told you it was good."

She took a sip of her water and glanced around the restaurant. The ski lodge was a sweet place and pretty swank. It had been closed down until about five years ago when the family had returned to town and renovated it. The restaurant had that resort lodge vibe with hardwood floors and exposed beams crisscrossing the ceiling. It also had the requisite floor-to-ceiling windows, and in this case, they looked out over the ski slopes.

The ski lodge was busy, seriously busy. It

had become the most popular one in this part of Alaska.

"You ever been downhill skiing?" I asked.

Skylar shook her head quickly, looking startled that I would ask.

"All right, we're going."

"I can't afford that."

"We have standing ski passes for the lodge. They send us business, and we send them business. I promise you won't have to pay a penny."

"How is it in the spring?"

I eyed the snowy peaks just outside. "We're at the top of the range, so there's still snow. Let's do it."

She chewed on her bottom lip, and my balls tightened in response. Fuck me. This woman had a direct line of electricity to my balls.

"Okay, but I have never been on a set of skis. Ever."

I bit back a smile. "It'll be fine. We'll do the bunny slope," I assured her.

Just then, Delia Hamilton paused by our table, catching the tail end of my comment. "The bunny slope is my favorite," she offered with a smile.

Skylar looked up at her, smiling shyly.

"I've never been skiing, and he's trying to tell me I should go."

"Even the bunny slope is fun, or you could do cross-country. That's fewer hills," Delia offered. "How was dinner?"

"Excellent. Always," I said firmly.

"Amazing," Skylar added.

"I'm Delia Hamilton, by the way," Delia said, holding her hand out.

Skylar shook it, replying, "I'm Skylar. I work out at the airport transport place."

"I heard. We're glad you finally made it up here to try our restaurant," she replied warmly.

"Delia is the chef for the lodge. She and Daphne could be competition, but they're friends instead," I explained.

Delia laughed lightly. "Of course, we are. Daphne's amazing. In all honesty, she's a better chef than me."

"Your food is excellent," Skylar insisted.

Delia grinned, lightly squeezing Skylar's shoulder. "I hope so. I wasn't professionally trained, but I've been a cook my whole life."

"Delia's family owns this lodge," I added.

"Not me," she returned.

"You married into it," I teased.

Delia grinned before shifting her focus to Skylar again, explaining, "Gage Hamilton is my brother-in-law. He returned to open the lodge after their parents closed it years ago. Marley, who you might have met at the reception desk, is his wife and does all the magic to make this place run. The rest of the family has mostly trickled back except for Becca. She's in Seattle, but she comes up a few times a year. She's our city connection. I'm married to Garrett, Gage's brother. He helps out here, and he's also a lawyer, so if you need any legal help, I can connect you to him."

"Well, I hope I won't need his help," Skylar replied.

Delia grinned. "You never know. He handles all kinds of legal cases, from criminal to property law and estate stuff. Anyway, it's very nice to meet you," she said warmly. "I hope we see more of you."

After she departed, Skylar asked, "Do you know everyone?"

"Definitely not," I deadpanned.

She rolled her eyes. "You know what I mean. Everywhere we go, people know you."

"This is a small town. It's hard for people not to know each other. Trust me, you will get to know most of the people in town. Maybe not everybody, but a lot."

She took another sip of her water. She'd

been looking worried all night, and I wanted to comfort her. I sensed if I were to even hint that I might notice her worry, she would shut the door on that conversation so fast my ears would ring from the slam of it. I kept telling myself I could manage this. We could have some kind of dating relationship, and she wouldn't matter too much.

I wanted her to believe people were worth trusting. Except the way I felt about Skylar was already opening doorways in my heart I hadn't known existed. When you fall in love when you're young, there's an innocence to it. When you're older and more jaded, there's something pure in a very different way about falling for someone.

Oh, I wasn't kidding myself. I wasn't in love with Skylar yet and didn't think I would ever fall in love. I knew how deep the blade could cut, so letting someone matter at all meant a lot.

When I got back to Skylar's place, I honestly wasn't thinking when I pulled around the back to park. It was only when I cut the engine and glanced sideways that I realized Skylar had noticed.

All evening, she'd given off a raw, touchy vibe. After what happened with Ludie, I understood. I wanted to fix everything for her.

"You checked on Ludie, right?" I asked.

"I texted. Dan said she's fine."

"I'm sure she will be."

The second those words came out, I realized that was total bullshit. There was never any certainty in life. Things went wrong, sometimes terribly, painfully wrong, and I knew that better than most. People who were healthy in the glow of their youth could be struck down. Ludie wasn't young. Maybe she would be fine tonight, or even for a little while. Yet there was one guarantee in life. We all died. At some point, her time would come.

As I stared into Skylar's worried gaze, I wasn't going to share that train of thought. The sound of my truck's engine cooling ticked in the quiet.

Skylar startled me by asking, "Do you want to come in?"

Chapter Twenty-Seven

SKYLAR

I wanted to tell myself I didn't know why I asked Tucker if he wanted to come in. Yet I knew exactly why.

I was feeling sharp along all my edges and soft as if my underbelly had been torn open and needed someone to make me feel better. This was my fallback when I was younger. Back when I was desperate for love and falling in love with every guy who came along. I had enough sense now to understand it wasn't really love. You could fall in love with the idea of love and feel like you were in love. That was what it was for me. That was how fiercely I craved the feeling.

For now, Tucker offered an escape I couldn't find alone. I missed Emily so much every day that it felt like a hole in my heart. I kept trying to patch it up. Some days, the hole felt stitched together, and other days, it was gaping open.

I was scared. I wasn't ready for something to happen to Ludie. Not yet. Because then I would be even more alone than I already was.

I didn't let out a sigh of relief when Tucker nodded. We walked up the stairs together. As hard as it was for me to make friends or let myself be emotionally vulnerable, the one place where I could be confident was sex. I threw myself into it. It was like a free ticket, a shortcut to intimacy, even if it wasn't the same.

When the door clicked shut behind us, I was already shimmying out of my jacket and kicking my boots off. Tucker watched me for a moment. He moved at a much slower pace. He shrugged out of his jacket, hung it, then carefully toed off one battered leather boot and then the other.

He was wearing a button-down over a T-shirt. As soon as he had that jacket off, I started pushing the shirt over his shoulders. It was flannel and soft to the touch. He caught my hands, saying, "Slow down."

I looked up at him, locked in his sky-blue

gaze. "I don't want to go slow." My voice came out raspy with an edge.

For a moment, I thought he was going to insist. That would make me feel more vulnerable than I already did. Even worse, though, he didn't insist. He whispered, "Okay."

Feeling exposed and split open, I pressed my hand to his chest, gratified to feel the thump of his heartbeat colliding with my palm. I leaned up to kiss him, pushing back.

Seconds later, his hips bumped into the couch. I tugged at the buttons on his fly. He was kissing the side of my neck, and everything felt rushed. I was caught in a tornado of sensation and need.

Tucker murmured, "Easy, Skylar."

But there was no easy. I needed this. I needed to lose myself in him. In us.

His palm skimmed down my side, trying to capture my hands, but I swatted them away. I shoved his jeans and boxers down just enough for his cock to spring free. I curled my palm around it, feeling it pulse under my touch, the skin hot and velvety soft.

Leaning down, I took his cock in my mouth, swirling my tongue around the tip and sucking lightly on the thick crown. Pre-cum danced across my tongue, the salty tang sliding down my throat. I sucked him in deeply, and his hand tangled in my hair. His touch was a little rough and just how I needed it right then.

He let out a growl, followed by a groan. I gripped his length with my palm, letting it slide up and down. I wanted him to feel like he couldn't control himself because I couldn't control myself. But his control was the only thing he didn't give me.

Just when I thought I might push him over the edge, he tugged on my hair, murmuring, "Skylar."

I drew back, peering up at him. My lips parted as my breath came in deep gulps.

"Come 'ere."

To my surprise, I did. I straightened, and he brushed my hair back from my face, cupping my cheeks as he stared into my eyes.

Emotion rose inside me, like the rush of a storm coming in off the ocean. The rhythmic push and pull, the land and the sea trading the power. I breathed in deeply.

Tucker took my mouth in a devouring kiss before spinning me around, his hands sliding down my sides. He reached around to the front of my waist, deftly unzipping my jeans. Fiery seconds burned by as he shoved them down around my hips and bent me over the back of the couch. The friction of my jeans banded around my knees heightened the sensations ricocheting through me.

I could feel my arousal, the dampness between my thighs. I didn't even know when that had happened. Whenever I spent time alone with Tucker, or at least of late, my arousal was always right on the edge, chafing me, something I couldn't shake free. I didn't want to shake it free. It frightened me with its ease and its power.

His fingers delved into my core, and I felt his palm slide up my back in a sure, soothing pass. "Easy," he murmured again.

Being with him *was* easy, so very easy. Somehow, his touch was comforting because I felt so out of control. His fingers disappeared. Seconds later, I felt the press of his arousal at my entrance. He took a breath as if adjusting himself, drawing back slightly and then pressing in slowly, inch by inch. The slow, thick glide of him filling me elicited a plea from me.

Chapter Twenty-Eight

TUCKER

The sound of Skylar saying my name nearly pushed me over the edge. I almost came. I liked to think I had more control than I did with her.

But with her, the second I felt her spiraling, I followed. It was a storm I couldn't slow, the waves crashing relentlessly. She was tight and slick, rippling around me as I filled her, seating myself deeply. Her hands were gripping the back of the couch. Her skin was warm under my palm as I slid it down her spine to grip one of her hips.

I laced my other hand in her hair and held still, scrambling for some control, any control. Having her jeans tight around her knees increased the friction where we were joined.

When I drew back and sank into her again, she arched her back, letting out a raw cry, followed by a whimper when I filled her deeply.

"Tucker," she gasped on a breath when I withdrew and surged to fill her yet again. "Please. More."

All I could do was give her that—faster and deeper—until I felt her trembling. Her release was threatening. I curled over her, reached around, and teased her swollen, needy clit, slick with her arousal. I savored when she pushed back into me, and I felt her channel clamp around me tightly. She came in a shaking rush, followed by a noisy sob. Her head bowed down as all of her trembled.

I followed her over as my release cracked like lightning inside me. Thunder followed in a stormy burst that I couldn't control. I curled around her as we shuddered together. Long moments later, I gathered my control and slowly straightened, belatedly realizing I hadn't worn a condom.

Now wasn't the time to panic, although I stiffened for a moment. Skylar instantly tensed and asked, "What?"

I answered honestly, "I forgot to wear a condom."

She glanced over her shoulder, saying,

"I'm on the pill. I promise you don't need to worry about anything. I'm kind of paranoid."

"About what?" I asked.

"I get tested every year, and I haven't had sex since my last round of tests." She was ever practical.

"Okay. I always wear a condom, so I've never worried about that."

She shrugged. "I've always been careful."

I nodded and slowly withdrew. Seconds later, she announced, "I'm gonna shower."

Seeing as I was headed to the bathroom, I paused. She gestured for me to follow. "Come with me."

Now *that* surprised me. Skylar and more of her was everything I wanted at this moment. I was discovering maybe I wanted this, and maybe she was giving more than I expected. But this was something she felt safe offering, and it didn't involve her heart.

I followed her into the shower after we stripped off the rest of our clothes. This time, I had her against the wall. The hot water pounded down around us when we came. After we toweled off, I expected her to kick me out again. She didn't.

She curled her hand around mine and tugged me into her bed. I knew she needed someone for tonight. I was that someone.

Chapter Twenty-Nine

SKYLAR

At daybreak, the first shafts of light filtered through my curtains. I came awake, my eyes flying open. I was warm, curled up against Tucker's side, pressed tightly as a barnacle. My knee was thrown over his thigh, and the rest of me was plastered to him. His breath came in deep, slow gusts. My chin was tucked against his shoulder, and my palm rested against his pecs.

Sheesh. He was all firm and warm under my touch. Recollections wrapped in sensations filled me. I suddenly felt intensely vulnerable. I almost scrambled away from him, but that would wake him up.

I needed to be sane and calm as I lay there, savoring not being alone. I thought this through and realized maybe I could do this. I knew how not to fall in love because I knew what wasn't love. Last night and how incredible it felt wasn't love. I used to fall in love with what wasn't love.

I would have boundaries and things. It would be easy.

I knew precisely when Tucker woke up because his breathing changed. He didn't even pretend to be asleep. He rolled his head sideways just as his eyes opened.

"Mornin'," he murmured, his voice gravelly and crushed along the edges from sleep.

"Good morning." A flush washed over me from head to toe.

"Are you going to kick me out now?" he asked bluntly as his lips curled in a slow grin.

Butterflies amassed in my belly. I felt all tingly with my skin prickly as I stared at him. I couldn't help it. I smiled. "No," I said, maybe a little too forcefully.

Then my stomach growled, which was perfect because I needed something to laugh about.

"Hungry?" he teased.

"Obviously," I deadpanned.

"Let's go get breakfast at Misty Mountain Café."

"Do you need to go home?" I prompted.

He shook his head. "I always have a change of clothing in my truck." When my eyes widened, he added, "Not because I spend the night with people all the time. If I get stuck somewhere, I have options. It's either in the plane or my truck. Right now, it's in my truck."

————

Cammi's pretty blue eyes bounced from me to Tucker and back again. I smiled and hoped I wasn't blushing too hard. I was accustomed to masking my internal state. When you grew up poor and wore almost the same thing every day and had to worry about whether or not your parents had enough spare change for laundry, you learned how to play it cool. Maybe I couldn't hide my blushes from Tucker, but I could hide them from Cammi.

Of course, as soon as that entire train of thought went through my brain, I winced internally. I trusted Cammi. She was really nice, and I sensed it would hurt her if she understood how much I tried to hide myself and how I felt from everyone. As soon as I thought that and started to beat myself up, Jolene's voice chimed in my brain, reminding me I tended to look for excuses to give myself a hard time. "So what?" I used to say to her.

She would say, "It matters. Would you talk to a friend the way you talk to yourself in your own head?"

I was aghast at that thought. Hell, I wouldn't talk to a complete stranger the way I talked to myself inside the privacy of my own thoughts.

"I have a new coffee flavor today," Cammi offered.

I couldn't help but grin. "What is it?"

"Chipotle dark chocolate."

"I'll take it. Just make it strong."

"How about you, Tucker?" she asked, waggling her eyebrows.

He looked a little sheepish as he replied, "I'm not into variety when it comes to coffee."

She blew him a kiss. "I know you're not. I like you exactly the way you are, Tucker. Most people have their favorite coffee drink and stick with that, or something seasonal," she explained as she began to get our coffees ready. "Skylar is a rare breed when it comes to her coffee."

"Am I really that rare?"

"Yeah, you'll try almost anything. I don't think you have any habits except you don't like it too sweet," she returned with a quick smile.

I shrugged. "I just want the caffeine, so I'm willing to take it however I can get it. Straight to the vein would work, except I'm scared of needles."

Just then, a handsome man stepped to the counter on Tucker's other side, responding to my comment with a shudder, "Oh, I hate needles. Needle phobia is a real thing."

The man appeared to know Cammi and Tucker. Tucker gestured to me as he slipped his arm around my waist, saying, "This is Skylar. She works with Ludie and Dan." He nudged his chin toward the man. "This is Garrett."

"Garrett Hamilton," the man said.

"Are you Delia's husband?" I asked.

"The very one. Have you met her? She's amazing," he said earnestly.

I couldn't help but laugh. He was so unabashed in his praise of her. "I have. I had dinner at the lodge last night. It was delicious."

"It's the best place in town. I mean, except Daphne's food is also amazing," he added quickly.

Cammi smiled. "There's no competition

between them. They're each other's biggest cheerleaders and what they do is different."

Garrett flashed a smile. "Working for Ludie and Dan must be interesting."

"It definitely is," I agreed.

"So you coordinate all the cargo scheduling for the small planes, right?" he prompted.

"Yup. It's never slow."

Garrett nodded. I suddenly connected the dots that he was a lawyer, and Susie had mentioned he could help me with any legal stuff around business planning if I looked into getting Ludie and Dan's business. I didn't have the nerve to ask him about it right now, so I stayed quiet.

A few minutes later, Tucker and I were sitting at a table by the windows, and I realized I hadn't been nervous with him. I'd had a normal conversation with Cammi and then a normal conversation with Garrett. I was just here with Tucker. I felt more normal than I'd ever imagined.

Tucker was chewing on a bite of his bagel. He swallowed before prompting, "What?"

"Nothing," I chirped.

"You were wondering something," he added, his lips teasing at the corners.

"Nobody's brain is just completely quiet," I countered.

I chewed on the inside of my cheek and took a swallow of coffee. It was so rare for me to have any span of time when I felt comfortable that it was almost a monumental event in my life.

The last time I'd had coffee and breakfast out in public and felt normal was before Emily died. We used to have our favorite coffee shop in San Francisco.

I ignored the beat of pain in my heart and took a sip of my drink, which was really good.

"I was just thinking it's nice to be here," I finally said.

Okay, that was like super general and vague, but sort of the truth.

He studied me before nodding.

It *was* nice to be here. I didn't even try to lie to myself about it. The only thing I lied to myself about—with fervor, by the way—was that I didn't really like Tucker. This was just a friendly arrangement. We liked each other naked, a lot. I let myself tumble into that, telling myself it wouldn't be a big deal.

Chapter Thirty

TUCKER

I was bone-tired a few nights later. Grant eyed me from where he sat at an angle across from me on the sectional at the staff house, commenting, "Well, you've made an appearance."

"What do you mean?"

"Just sayin'. I haven't seen you in a few nights."

"Yeah, same can be said for you. Have you been home every night?"

He shook his head slowly. "But I'm not usually home every night. You are. Hell, you lead a boring life."

Harley sat over at a small table by the windows with her laptop. She was always doing some kind of graphic design project.

She called over, "He doesn't lead a boring life. He flies planes all over Alaska. That's a career many people would envy. I'm surprised there's not a reality show on it." Her hands stilled on her keyboard as she glanced back and forth between us. "Oh, my god, I'm gonna propose that."

"Propose what?" Grant prompted.

"There should be a pilot reality show, Alaskan style. Would you guys go for it?" she asked.

"Are you fucking insane?" Grant's eyes went wide. "Plus, we're not the right group. None of us cares about how we look. And except for me, you, and Tucker, everybody's paired up, which means no drama. I am not signing on to something that involves people breaking up, especially Flynn or Nora," he said, shaking his head.

"Oh, so you'd rather see Elias or Diego break up?" I teased.

Grant glared at me. "Are you serious? Do you remember how fucking cranky Flynn was before he settled down with Daphne, and then Nora and Gabriel? Not only were they going to kill each other but I thought we were all going to kill them. I'm not saying their relationships are more valuable. I'm just saying I appreciate the peace around here."

"Diego and Elias would be just as miserable and cranky if their relationships ended," Harley chimed in. "Plus, it doesn't have to be a reality show about sex and romance and drama. It's about flying in Alaska." She spun in her chair, tapping on her keyboard again.

Grant looked back at me. "No one wants a pilot show."

I shrugged. "Maybe, maybe not."

"So how is Skylar?" he asked.

I wasn't hiding from anyone that I'd been with her. But I also wasn't ready to talk about it. At least, not much. I was working damn hard to convince myself this was no big deal. I just wanted her to know not all men were assholes. It wasn't going to go anywhere. I wasn't going to fall for her.

Liar, liar. My critical mind taunted me, and I ignored it.

Just then, my cell phone vibrated on the coffee table. I leaned over to snag it, glancing down. I was startled to see a text from my dead high school girlfriend's mother.

Tucker, I hope this message finds you well. She was forever polite, apparently even in a text message. *I'm texting to let you know that I'm going to be sending you a letter from Claire. I didn't want it to startle you. I hope you're doing well in life. We miss you, and I know your parents miss you. Love, Teresa.*

I almost couldn't feel anything for a minute. Then my heart was clanging in my chest as if a stormy wind was blowing, clattering a bell wildly.

I hadn't heard from anyone in Claire's family in a while. They texted here and there. I must've stared at my phone too long. I almost forgot where I was.

Grant's voice punctured my thoughts. "You okay?"

My head whipped up, and I gave it a little shake, letting out a breath. "Yeah, fine."

"You look like you've seen a fucking ghost, dude."

"Does my dead girlfriend's mom qualify as a ghost?" I asked bluntly.

"What?! What happened?" Harley glanced over, her brow knitting with worry.

"It was a long time ago. She died from Ewing's sarcoma. Freaking brutal."

"Do you want to talk about it?" Grant asked slowly.

I had to give the guy some credit. He was so obviously uncomfortable, but he was a decent guy, and he wanted to support me if I wanted to talk about it.

"Nah, it's been a long time, and I'm okay,

but thank you." I wasn't up for responding to that text just now, so I closed the screen and went upstairs to bed.

My mind played tennis in my brain, bouncing between thoughts of Claire and Skylar. It was strange to think about Claire now. I had loved her, I really had. It was just that when you were that young, it was hard to know how things would've gone. Back then, I believed we would be together forever. When she got sick, I was positive she would beat the odds. I learned then the odds were usually right. The odds for Ewing's sarcoma are cruel. Absolutely brutal.

All this time, I told myself I never wanted to love someone and lose them again. I didn't believe that bullshit about "it's better to have loved and lost than never have loved at all." It really wasn't. Fuck that noise. Yet here was Skylar. I wanted her to believe love was worth fighting for. What the hell was I doing?

Chapter Thirty-One

SKYLAR

We didn't discuss it, but somehow, Tucker and I both knew we couldn't spend every night together. I meant for this thing with us to be a casual, low-key, purely sexual relationship. Yet he was already slipping through cracks in the walls around my heart. Walls I'd thought were impenetrable.

The sex was good, so very good, and so easy to lose myself in. After a few nights of hot, hot, hot with him, I mentioned I was going to the yoga class in town. Tucker said he had something to take care of out at the lodge. It was that simple.

I found myself silently talking to Emily about it, pointing out that she'd be proud of me because I wasn't falling apart inside. I wasn't being needy and clingy. That part was true. Maybe that was the only thing I'd ever needed to figure out to begin with, that I shouldn't be so grabby about love. I should take what I could get. In this case, that was one hot sexy man and a few hot nights. No breakup necessary.

I knew that wasn't the end, though.

The minute I stepped through the door at Gemma's yoga studio, she smiled over at me. Her rumpled curls swung around her shoulders when she straightened from where she'd been folding towels. "Hey there," she called.

I waved, suddenly feeling uncertain. "I'm here for the yoga class."

"And I'm so grateful you're here." Her voice was warm, and she had a little spark in her eyes.

"Am I the first person here?"

"You are—"

Before she even finished her sentence, the chime rang above the door, and a cluster of women entered. I didn't recognize any of them. Gemma smoothed her hand across my shoulder in a light caress as she walked by.

"Put your mat down wherever you'd like. I have mats and towels up front. They're all clean. Just grab one. You can put your things in a cubby and pick a spot."

She began greeting the women who'd entered. After fetching a mat from the shelves, I heard a voice I recognized and glanced over to see Daphne, Cat, and Nora coming in.

Daphne saw me first, her eyes lighting up with her smile. "Well, hey, I know exactly where we're gonna be."

I looked around the room as Cat waved and skipped toward me. "Hey, it's like class. You want to be beside the people you like."

Her comment, so simple and probably meant in a teasing, casual manner on her part, meant so much to me. Emotion welled inside.

A moment later, Cat spread her mat on the floor beside me, and Daphne with Nora on the other side of Cat. We didn't have much time to chat before Gemma started class.

Emily and I had gone to yoga classes together, but they were free. Through an independent living program that had funding for us after we aged out of foster care. This class was on the vigorous side. By the time it was over, I was more than grateful to lay on my back and zone out. Gemma counted down, her voice soothing. I let myself actually be quiet inside my thoughts.

A few minutes later, it shifted from complete silence to soft music as Gemma instructed the class to leave when we were ready. I rolled over and sat crisscross as I looked around the classroom. People started to get up and leave.

Daphne smiled at me. "Want to go get dinner with us?"

I said, "Sure," before I really thought it through.

"Yay!" Cat said, lifting her hands in a mini cheer.

"Where are we going?" I asked.

Daphne cocked her head to the side, drumming her fingertips on her knees. "I don't know. We can always grab dinner at Misty Mountain Café, or we could go to Sally's. Have you been to Sally's?"

I shook my head when she met my eyes. "Well, then, let's go there."

"I thought it was a bar."

"It is, but they also have a restaurant. It's good too. I think every town should be required to have a bar that has good pub fare," she replied.

I nodded as though I knew what pub fare was. Roughly half an hour later, Daphne cast me what seemed like a benign smile. I quickly discovered otherwise.

"So you and Tucker?" she commented, her voice lilting with a question.

"Um, yeah?"

"Just wondering how it's going," she prompted, her smile holding.

Girl talk. This was the thing I didn't know how to navigate. I'd only had girl talk with one friend, and she was gone.

"I think it's just casual right now," I finally said.

"I don't think so," Daphne returned.

Cat looked up from her phone where she was texting with a friend. "Tucker likes you. A lot." Her eyes returned to her phone screen as her thumbs tapped away.

Nora cast me a sympathetic smile. "If you didn't notice yet, this group has opinions on love lives. Daphne has made it her personal mission to make sure everybody she cares about falls in love."

"You and Gabriel are doing great, aren't you?" Daphne countered.

Nora's cheeks flushed pink with her smile. "Yes, we are. Thank you very much."

Daphne practically preened as she straightened in the booth before leaning back. "Everybody deserves a chance at love." Her eyes swung to me again, and I nodded.

I took another bite of my burger. I had learned pub fare was basically burgers and fries. When I got home later that night, I did my usual routine of watching TV and then turning everything off. After that, I stared out the windows over the dark ocean rippling under the reflection from the moon and stars glittering in the sky.

I didn't feel as lonely as I had before. Emily was still gone and always would be, but I was making friends, sort of. I tried not to think about missing Tucker that night. I missed his presence, though. A lot.

When my brain wouldn't shut up about it, I told myself it was just because the sex was so great. My body missed him. Not my heart.

Bullshit, my good angel whispered.

Chapter Thirty-Two

SKYLAR

"Today's the day," Tucker announced as he got out of his truck after I'd climbed out of my car.

The sun was just rising. The world felt quiet and almost brimming with life. An eagle called, followed by the chatter of a magpie. The gust of wind coming off Kachemak Bay was brisk. I could smell the briny tang in the air as my hair swirled in the breeze. The sky was lavender with the silvery rays of the sun shooting through it.

"Today's the day for what?" I zipped my jacket up as I stuffed my hands in my pockets, my lips automatically curling into a smile as I looked up at him.

Tucker was the kind of man who elicited

a smile. His curly brown hair was still a bit damp, and his blue eyes seemed especially bright this morning, matching the sky.

"The day I'm taking you up for a plane ride," he explained.

"I have to work."

"I thought ahead and asked Ludie. I told her I wanted to take you for a ride, and she said any day."

"You asked Ludie?" I yelped.

Tucker shrugged, all easy breezy about it. "Yeah, why not? Even she agreed that you need to take a trip into the sky here."

I stared up at him, thinking about Emily and how she died. I remembered what I'd promised her. "Um, okay. When?"

"Well, I'm on a delivery run today. Since it's just cargo, you can ride in the front. It's perfect."

"How long, though?" I ignored the anxiety clenching in my belly and around my heart.

He glanced at his watch. "Probably two hours."

I opened my mouth to say I couldn't take that much time away from work, but he cut in, "Before you say no, check with Ludie."

I eyed him and nodded slowly, thinking he didn't realize he'd just given me an out.

She'd say that was too much time to be out of the office.

"I'll be over in the hangar. I need to take care of a few things before I fly."

Just as I started to turn away, he caught me lightly by the elbow. When I spun back to face him, he was right there, his blue eyes boring into mine. "I forgot something," he said.

"What?"

"This." He bent low, bringing his lips to mine.

The hot shock of it startled me. I felt him smile against my mouth, then he lingered for a moment before lifting his head. "Good to see you, Skylar."

My heart was stumbling, carelessly casting out beats. As I stared up at him, my belly swooped. And I knew, I just *knew*, down to my bones, this man could break my heart in a way it had never been broken before. Yet the giddiness of that kiss, of him being happy to see me, elbowed my fears away. Before I could even absorb everything, he was turning and calling over his shoulder, "Talk to you in a few."

I hurried across the parking lot and into the office. I skidded to a stop in front of

Ludie's office, and she smiled up at me. "Morning, Skylar. You should go."

"Huh?"

"With Tucker. I just saw you two talking."

"Oh. Are you sure? He said it'll be about two hours."

"Of course, I'm sure. And you're still getting paid."

"But, Ludie, I won't be working," I protested.

"Consider it training. I didn't know you actually hadn't been up in one of the small planes yet. I assumed you had."

Shaking my head slowly, I thought about Emily broken and bleeding after her plane crash.

"Go. It actually is part of this job to know what it feels like for those guys to be up in the air. You'll see why the schedule can get all wonky when the weather messes things up." At my doubtful look, she pressed, "Go, sweetie. Dan's already got it covered."

Without thinking, I uncurled my hand from the doorframe, then raced around her desk and leaned down to give her a hug. I squeezed her tight. "Thank you, Ludie."

My throat ached as I straightened.

"You got it, hon," she said gruffly and waved me out of her office.

I didn't leave just yet and hurried down the hallway to check with Dan. "Ludie said you've got it covered if I go for a flight with Tucker. Are you sure that's okay?"

Dan looked up at me, his weathered face cracking a smile. "Of course, it's okay. Neither of us knew you hadn't flown yet. If I was still in my heyday, I'd insist on being the one to take you up there."

Dan used to fly. That was why Ludie started this business all those years ago. He'd stopped flying over a decade back. According to him, it was after he had a problem with his eyesight. Even though he'd had surgery and improved, he said he didn't want to worry about it.

"Scram," he added with a wink.

I wasn't quite ready to hug Dan, so I smiled and hurried back out of the office. I told myself it didn't mean anything that Tucker offered to do this as I jogged across the parking lot. Walker Adventures owned or rented a number of the hangars here, but I knew where he was. I remembered Emily saying she only ran when somebody chased her. I was smiling when I slowed.

Tucker glanced over. "What are you smiling about?"

I came to an abrupt stop, the sound of my

footsteps skidding on the concrete and echoing in the space. "My friend Emily," I said honestly.

"It's good to have good memories."

"It is."

I was coming to realize that grief changed over time. At first, the edges were sharp, every edge practically a razor slicing over your heart. You didn't know which way to adjust so the pain wasn't so brutal. Over time, the edges got a little duller. Sometimes, you could recall a good memory, and your heart would feel warm. It would feel like you were carrying a piece of that person inside you. That was how I felt just then. Maybe Emily and I planned this move together, and maybe I was doing it for her. My persistence and grit had carried me through it even though I had almost fallen into an inertia like no other after she died.

I was becoming someone new here. I was still me, but I was finding my fresh start.

"What's the word? What did Ludie say?" Tucker asked.

"She said it was fine. Dan said if he still flew, he would have already taken me up."

Tucker chuckled. "I'm sure he would have. I don't know why he stopped flying."

My feet finally moved again, and I

crossed over to stop beside the plane. Tucker was putting something in the small compartment under the plane. "He had cataracts, so he took a break. Then he had some complications from the surgery. I guess it's all sorted out now, but he said he didn't want to worry about it," I explained.

"I can't say I blame him. I love flying like it's my life, and I can't imagine doing anything else for work." Tucker was so serious that it felt as if he was speaking spiritually about flying. "But it's important to feel like you're one-hundred-percent, all cylinders firing—sight, sound, reflexes. I think I'll do the same thing when the time comes."

I nodded. Because, of course, that made sense. "Can I do anything to help?"

"Nope. You can hop in, though. We'll taxi out from here."

I couldn't help the fizzy hum of anticipation spinning inside. This was exciting. I couldn't wait to see what Alaska looked like from the air.

Moments later, Tucker handed me a headset and told me which channel to put it on. "Oh, this is the channel where you guys talk, and I don't get to hear you."

He grinned. "We don't use it that much.

This is just for you and me to chat. You ready?"

I met his eyes, and it felt as if the air shifted. Something shimmered to life between us. It wasn't about desire or lust. I didn't even recognize what it was about. I would only realize that later. My heart felt full, and excitement tumbled through me, like water rushing over the rocks in the spring. I nodded.

He taxied to the end of the runway. Before I could think about it too long, we were airborne.

"Oh, wow," I breathed as I scanned the landscape beneath us.

"I know," Tucker replied. "Simply beautiful, isn't it?"

That word didn't seem big enough. I'd seen Alaska from land, but this bird's-eye view was stunning. Kachemak Bay was sparkling under the sun, and the light glinted like sparks where the waves ruffled the surface. When I looked out in the distance and saw Mount Augustine, my breath caught. The sky was clear, and the volcano was tall and dark, its powerful presence almost alive.

I fell silent as Tucker flew. There were a few gusts of wind, and it felt like what I imagined it would feel like to be in a clothes dryer. When wind buffeted the plane, he steadied it. Before one of his stops, he flew low along the edge of the water, pointing out a cluster of rocks where a herd of sea lions was sunning themselves.

"Ooh!" I squeaked when I saw one swimming underwater, its form large and dark.

"Sometimes we see bears, plenty of seals and moose too."

I helped him unload at the two stops. Then as promised, he delivered me back to Diamond Creek, almost two hours later.

"How many more flights do you have?" I asked after we'd climbed out of the plane.

He glanced at his phone, commenting, "Three. All tourist trips."

"Thank you for today," I said, my heart tightening in my chest.

"Of course."

He startled me again when he bent low and kissed me. He lingered just long enough to tease his tongue with mine. Just that had me breathless by the time he lifted his head.

He waved. "I'll text you."

I hurried into work, realizing as I put on my headset that I'd finally kept my small promise to Emily.

Chapter Thirty-Three

TUCKER

I was trying to play it cool—*really* trying—but I was failing. Completely. I didn't know if it was Skylar or me. Probably both. It felt so different to fall for her than it had with Claire. Back then, I'd been young and foolish. Not foolish for falling for Claire, but just not realizing the way life could go. When I was young and in high school, I'd pretty much thought I would live forever.

Until death and loss came slapping me in the face with a force so hard my ears rang from it for years.

That evening, without thinking, my feet aimed toward Ludie and Dan's office. It was quiet when I walked into the front area, and I called out, "Anybody here?"

The front entrance offered a view down the hallway. Skylar peered out from a doorway. "Hey, I'm just shutting everything down."

"Can I come back?"

"Sure." She disappeared through the doorway.

I walked down the hallway, my heart rolling into a thundering beat. She was leaning over the desk, turning off computer screens.

"Was I the last flight to land tonight?"

She glanced up with a quick smile and nodded.

"My deliveries were on time at least."

She laughed. "You usually are."

I leaned my shoulder against the doorway, watching as she looked around before nodding as if satisfied everything was turned off. "All good?" I asked.

"Yeah." She snagged her purse off a chair, lifting the keys beside it. "I didn't know you were stopping by."

"I didn't either," I answered honestly.

Her cheeks were tinged pink when she looked up at me. I couldn't resist slipping an arm around her waist and pulling her against me as I stepped closer.

"How was your day?" I murmured, my lips a whisper away from hers.

"Pretty good. Yours?"

"Same."

Then I was kissing her. I didn't know for how long, but by the time we broke apart, I was rock hard and aching for her.

She stared up at me, her lips kiss swollen and her eyes wide. "You can't do that," she rasped.

"I can't?"

"Somebody might see."

"No one's looking, Skylar."

She laughed softly. "Fair enough."

"Can I come home with you?"

We stared at each other, her eyes searching mine. For a second, I thought she was going to say no.

Then she whispered, "Yes."

Chapter Thirty-Four

SKYLAR

Against my better judgment, Tucker stayed with me for another three nights. That seemed to be our rhythm. I suppose everything came in threes. In our case, we fell into a pattern of spending three nights together followed by three nights apart.

It was almost a joke, and we didn't talk about it. By silent agreement, it was as if we had decided that meant we weren't being stupid about us.

I didn't know what he felt. I knew *I* was being stupid. That old familiar feeling, that desperation for someone to love me, was starting to build inside. All the while, I kept trying to tell myself I didn't need to let myself go there.

After a third night apart, I went to a yoga class at the lodge because Daphne invited me. I'd fallen into the habit anyway, so it wasn't unusual, or that was what I told myself. I expected that Tucker expected me to be there at this point. But he wasn't in class that night. I told myself not to wonder about it, yet a funny feeling started to spin inside my belly.

Uneasiness tangled with so many doubts and so much uncertainty. If I was certain about one thing in life, it was that I would be abandoned. I would not be wanted.

I told myself it wouldn't matter if we didn't have three more nights together. We would be friends, and it would be fine.

If my heart were a container, it had been punctured and was leaking blood, doubt, and the bitter acid of regret for letting myself be so stupid.

After dinner, Daphne smiled over at me. "I'm not sure where Tucker is tonight. Do you know?"

Shaking my head, I hoped she couldn't sense my internal turmoil. "Well, I'll find out," she said firmly.

I managed to smile at that. "Tucker and I are just friends."

My heart didn't think we were, but I thought that was technically the truth.

I drove home later and thought about texting him but decided against it. What would I say?

Where are you? It's been three nights apart. We're now supposed to start three nights together.

It all just felt ridiculous, and we didn't have these conversations. That was the silent agreement we'd made.

I had a restless night of sleep, which wasn't unusual. Most of my life had been shitty nights of sleep. Living with uncertainty was part of that, at least in my world.

The following morning, I decided to go to Red Truck Coffee. I told myself I wasn't expecting to see Tucker there, that I stopped there anyway because it was on the way to work. Maybe that was splitting hairs, but those were all the things I told myself until I got in line and felt the hairs on the back of my neck rise when I heard a vehicle turn into the parking area.

It's just tires on gravel, I told myself. *It's not Tucker. It could be anybody.*

The coffee truck was busy. I was at the back of the line, and five people were in front of me. I wouldn't even let myself look at all until the very last second when I glanced over my shoulder, all casual-like, and there he was.

Tucker smiled, but it didn't quite reach his eyes. When he said, "Good morning," he sounded normal, but I sensed something was off.

"Good morning."

"Sorry I missed yoga class last night," he offered.

"I didn't expect you to be there." I didn't. I *really* didn't. Lying to myself was an effective coping strategy, even if it wasn't healthy.

His brows hitched incrementally at that reply. "I'll be there next week," he added.

"I'm not sure if I'll be there."

"Daphne invites you every week now," he countered.

We weren't quite arguing, but it sort of felt like it. All over a stupid yoga class.

I mentally decided I probably wouldn't go to yoga out at the lodge next week. I needed this thing with Tucker and me to stay compartmentalized. Maybe if he showed up tonight or texted about stopping by, I might be busy. That would be a lie, but still, it was the best thing for both of us.

He commented on the weather and asked if I was going to work. Of course, I said yes

because I was. I insisted on getting his coffee.
I reminded him I owed him one, and he
didn't argue. When we parted, he didn't surprise me with a kiss. I told myself I wasn't
disappointed. Not even a tiny bit.

Chapter Thirty-Five

TUCKER

The plane hangar was quiet after I did my final checks and closed the garage bay door. I walked into the small office, if one could call it that, in the back corner. It was a small square room with a bathroom and a desk. It was entirely utilitarian. We had some shelving on the wall, where we kept odds and ends.

I sank into the chair at the desk and reached into my jacket pocket, pulling out the crumpled envelope. Claire's handwriting was so familiar. My heart felt stung as if something ragged with sharp, hard edges had scraped across the surface of it.

It wasn't a mortal wound, but it hurt like hell.

Dear Tucker,

It should have been fifteen years now. You're 32, and I hope you're happy. I hope you're not upset that I asked my parents to hold on to this and send it later. I wanted to wait so that you had time to get past us. Maybe I haven't reached eighteen yet, but I've already figured out people are kind of confused. We don't know what we want, not really, when we're young. I think by now maybe you know what you want. I hope you followed your dream into the Air Force and that you're flying planes somehow. I don't know where. I know you're good at it. You're so detail-oriented. I also hope you've fallen in love again. You should be about to get married if you're not already.

Mostly what I wanted to say was that I feel so lucky. I got to love you and have you love me. I don't feel like life is fair. In this case, I feel like it's more unfair to you than me. Oh, don't get me wrong, I'm downright furious that I'm dying. I'm writing this today before they think I'll die. I'm pretty weak, but I'm bored too, so I might as well write.

You love hard, and you're so loyal, but I'm worried about one thing. I hope you didn't let me getting sick and dying make you bitter. I already see some of that. You're angry. Not at me, but at the universe. Don't do that. Please. Please give love a chance. Do it for me.

Thank you for loving me as much as you did. Many people would have walked away from this, but you didn't. That tells me what kind of man you are. You're already one of the strongest people I know, and I hope it only makes you stronger.

I love you. I'm blowing you a kiss.

Claire

p.s. Please burn this. Don't cling to a piece of paper.

My eyes blurred as I stared down at the letter, the teardrops falling just below her writing. The salty tears didn't stain her words, but they marred the surface of the paper. This was written on lavender paper, her favorite color. It wasn't lined, but Claire's writing was tidy.

I took a shaky breath and glanced around, laughing through my tears when I realized there wasn't a box of tissues here. I set her letter on the desk and crossed into the bathroom, grabbing some toilet paper off the roll. I blew my nose, wiped my eyes, and sat down, reading through the letter once again and wondering just what the fuck to do.

Claire had been right. I *was* bitter. She would have liked Skylar. I knew she would. Yet I couldn't deal with facing Skylar right now.

Claire wanted me to burn this letter, this

last piece of her. What the fuck? What. The. Fuck.

What was I supposed to do? I couldn't burn this. It was all I had of Claire. Yet that love felt a million miles away right now. A corner of my heart was reserved for her. My heart was bigger for it, which was why I was afraid.

———

That night, I texted Skylar. She didn't reply.

The following morning, I saw her at Red Truck Coffee. She smiled politely from where she stood ahead of me in line.

When I stopped by Ludie and Dan's office that evening, Skylar said she had plans, which I suspected was a lie.

I texted her the next day, and she replied as vaguely as possible with: *Busy. Hope you're doing okay.*

She even included a smiley emoticon, which was so not like her that I knew it was bullshit.

All the while, I missed her. I still hadn't burned Claire's letter. One night after staff dinner at the lodge, Daphne caught me lightly by the elbow as I was passing by the kitchen sinks.

"Yeah?" I prompted.

"Oh, I was just thinking you could help with the dishes," she said.

I looked around, and Cat caught my eye right before she practically raced out the door into the hallway in the back. There was no one else left in the kitchen. I was pretty sure I'd been set up to help Daphne clean. I eyed her suspiciously but nodded.

She started rinsing dishes and handing them to me, directing me to put them in a large industrial-style dishwasher. After we worked quietly for a few minutes, Daphne said, "I wanted an excuse to talk to you."

"Well, just say you want to talk to me," I replied, uncertainty churning in my gut.

I told myself this was just Daphne, and she was my friend. Except Daphne had this weird radar where she knew, like seriously knew, when something was up with you. We all joked about it. Flynn didn't worry about it because he loved her.

I kept putting the dishes in the dishwasher until it was full. I slid the rack in and tapped the button to start it before turning and resting my hips against the counter. "Just get to it. What's up?"

Daphne dried her hands on a towel before facing me. "You seem sad, and you haven't been seeing Skylar."

I leaned my head back, looking at the ceiling as I took a deep breath. Leveling my eyes with hers, I said, "How do you know I haven't been seeing Skylar?"

"Because I asked Harley and Grant, and you've been at the staff house every night." Daphne was unabashed in her nosiness.

"Oh, for fuck's sake," I burst out. "Are you guys talking about me?"

"Yeah, we're worried."

"We?"

"Okay, me," she said. "Just me. Everybody else says you'll figure it out at your own pace, but I think I'm the only one you talked to about what happened to your high school girlfriend."

I eyed the floor, tracing the toe of my boot along the edges of a square tile. "They know."

"They say you don't talk about it."

"I talked to you about it," I offered when I looked at her again.

Daphne let out a soft sigh. She took a step closer and wrapped her arms around me, pulling me into a warm hug. Even though she was only maybe five feet tall, if I was being generous, it felt like being hugged by my mother. Her embrace contained nothing but comfort. She stepped back, squeezing my shoulders lightly before her arms dropped away. "Do you want some hot chocolate with peppermint liqueur?"

I chuckled. Then of course, I thought of Skylar. She made me hot chocolate on that rainy night. "Sure, I don't have to drive anywhere. When you make spiked hot chocolate, you do not mess around."

"Of course not," Daphne said, clucking as she turned away. "So what's going on?"

"I got a letter from Claire."

Daphne glanced back at me, her eyes wide. "I thought—"

"She wrote it before she died when she was in the hospital. She asked the family attorney to hold it and give it to me after fifteen years, so they sent it to me."

"What did it say?"

I quickly summarized it for Daphne as she prepped hot chocolate. She handed me a mug after she poured a liberal helping of peppermint liqueur in it.

"It seems like she knew you very well," Daphne said, her words pointed but her eyes warm.

Just then, the door to the back hallway opened, and Flynn came walking through.

He took us in, his lips curling in a slow smile.

"Are you telling Tucker what to do?" he asked as he approached Daphne, stopping beside her and leaning down to drop a kiss on the side of her neck. Pink bloomed on her cheeks, and she smiled. "I'm not telling him what to do."

"She's worried about you," Flynn said dryly as he caught my eyes.

I chuckled. "I know. I'm fine."

"She's usually right, you know."

"How do you even know what she's talking about?"

Flynn shrugged nonchalantly. "That was a blanket statement. I don't have to know what Daphne's talking about to know she's usually right."

I rolled my eyes, but I knew he had a point. Daphne had been through some shit in her life. As a result, she tended to hone in quickly on what mattered.

"Hey, do I get some hot chocolate?" Flynn glanced at the saucepan on the stove.

There was no such thing as packaged hot chocolate in this kitchen. Daphne kept batches she made cool in the refrigerator and reheated them.

"Of course, I knew you were going to show up any minute," she teased with a smile.

Flynn filled a mug after she handed him one from a cabinet. He leaned his hips against the counter beside her before he looked over at me. "For what it's worth, you were in a better mood for a little while there."

"I'm not that bad," I protested.

"No, but you were kind of cheerful. I like Skylar."

"Oh, for fuck's sake. How do you even know what we're talking about?"

"Actually, I don't. Just a good guess, but you proved my point."

Flynn was one of my best friends and the very reason I was here, doing a job I loved with people I loved.

"Your sister called. I forgot to tell you," Daphne added.

"She did? When?"

"She says you don't call her back, but that if she leaves me a message, you usually do," Daphne replied, cocking her head to the side with a sly grin.

I sighed. "I don't mean to not call her back. I just get busy, and it slips my mind. I promise, I'll call her."

Flynn wisely shifted the topic away from

Skylar, and we chatted about a few plane issues we were dealing with and the ever-
present stress. We were facing the good
problem of having too many bookings. We
were already booked for the entire summer
with tourist flights.

A short while later, I slipped my phone
out of my pocket as I walked out into the
darkness to call my sister back. She answered
on the first ring.

"Oh, good. Daphne passed on my
message."

"Of course, she did. Sorry I haven't called
sooner, Tori. I don't mean to blow you off
when you leave me messages, but I forget."

"I know, but you have guilt. I've discovered that when it comes to Daphne, I get
results."

I chuckled. "How's it going?"

"Good, how are you?" my sister asked.

I thought about Skylar and the letter
from Claire. "Pretty good."

As far as the basics—food, clothing, shel-
ter, and living—I was pretty good. I didn't
need a love life, or so I'd told myself for
years.

"Did you get the letter? Claire's parents
mentioned they sent it to you."

My sister had been friendly with Claire. I

should have known she knew about the letter.

I silently groaned. Just then, I heard a loud rustling sound and came to a quick stop, glancing around. Moonlight fell through the canopy of trees, casting the landscape with a pearly glow. I saw the shadow of a moose lumbering away from me, already a safe distance away.

I resumed walking. "How do you know about the letter?"

"I ran into Claire's mom at the doctor's office, of all places. She mentioned that they didn't even know about the letter either. It was left with the attorney who handled everything. The attorney was instructed to keep it private. You're not the only one who got a letter."

"You got one?"

"Her parents did. I did."

"What was yours about?"

Tori sighed softly. "Not getting cynical, not letting what happened in high school screw up my life."

"Do you want to talk about it?" I asked.

"No," she said quickly enough that I knew her old friend had hit a sore spot.

My sister had her own baggage. We didn't talk about it much, almost never.

"What was yours about?" she pressed.

"Not getting bitter. Oh, and I'm supposed to burn the letter. Are you supposed to burn yours?"

"Uh, no."

"Why am I supposed to burn mine?" I muttered.

"Because you and Claire were in love. It was the real thing, and it was freaking high school. She knew you well enough to know that if you keep it, you'll still be holding on to her, and she's dead." Tori didn't shy away from being blunt, but I heard the pain in her voice.

"I know."

"You need to honor her wishes," she added firmly.

"I will."

"Do you think she's right?" my sister asked softly.

I bit back a sigh. "Probably. I met someone."

"You did? Who? Tell me about her."

The clearing in front of the staff house opened through the trees. A soft glow cast in a circle from the porch light. I crossed over and sank my hips onto the stairs.

I told her about Skylar. And after I finished, Tori said, "Tucker, I think you're already in love."

"What?" My heart lunged, kicking hard, as if about to break down a locked door.

"I'm just saying, it's the way you talk about her."

"Aw, fuck," I muttered.

"She sounds nice," my sister protested.

"I don't think relationships come easy to her after what she went through." As if my guardedness didn't have anything to do with my reaction.

"Tucker, relationships don't come easy to anyone. Everybody has baggage and gets banged up by life. What you had in high school with Claire probably came easy just because you were so young. Falling in love after you've been through some shit is different, and in a way, it's more powerful. I'm not saying falling in love again will ever take away from what you had with Claire, but you have the chance to have so much more now. Loving someone else doesn't make another love grow smaller. It only makes it bigger. Love isn't finite."

I stayed silent, absorbing her words.

"I think you know you're in love with Skylar," she insisted.

I wanted to protest, but I didn't.

She shifted the conversation to lighter topics, and a few minutes later, we ended the call. I sat on the stairs, looking up into the sky scattered with stars dazzling in the darkness. I knew I loved Skylar. I just didn't know what to do with the feeling.

———

A full six days passed before I saw Skylar again. If I'd been doubting whether or not I loved her, I didn't doubt it anymore. I missed her like crazy. I wanted to see her and hold her. Sure, I missed the sex, which was fiery hot, but that wasn't what kept my heart aching.

I had texted her only twice, and her replies were vague enough that I gave her space. Even though I wanted to press for more, I'd come to understand her and knew any pressure from me would only chase her away.

Chapter Thirty-Six

SKYLAR

I was an expert at avoidance, and I made myself invisible for an entire week. Daphne invited me out to the lodge for the staff dinner, and I told her I was busy. That was total bullshit because my social life was nonexistent without my new friends, but whatever.

I went into work early so I didn't accidentally run into Tucker at Red Truck Coffee or Misty Mountain Café. I made sure to lock the door at the office at the end of the day when Ludie and Dan left, so nobody could just stop in. I also turned out all the lights in the front.

One evening, there was a knock on the glass doors. I didn't dare look out because I knew it was Tucker. I waited and waited.

When I heard the scuff of footsteps moving away on the gravel, I tiptoed over and peered out from the hallway. My heart felt pierced when I saw the back of him moving slowly away. He glanced over his shoulder, and I darted back.

Leaning against the wall, I slid my hips to the ground, curled my knees to my chest, and wrapped my arms around them as I let my forehead fall. I cried and cried and cried. I didn't think I was just crying about Tucker although the ache of missing him was sharp. I cried because I missed Emily, and she would never come back. I cried because it didn't feel like life was fair. I cried because I tried not to be the kind of person who counted all the things that had gone wrong and kept track, but I felt like I'd been doled out more than enough of the shitty luck. Maybe, just maybe, the tide could turn.

And I cried because even though I knew better, I'd gone and fallen in love with Tucker, and I didn't know what to do about it.

He had texted me a few times, and I blithely replied, profoundly grateful he couldn't see my face or the scorched surface of my heart. I didn't know why he'd kept his distance for those few days, but it reminded me of all the reasons I never ever, *ever*, should've let anything happen with him.

I finally stopped crying and lifted my head before dragging my sleeve across my face. I sat there on the floor in the utilitarian office and slowly got my breath back. I jumped when there was another knock out front.

Fuck. I didn't want to deal with Tucker, but this knock was determined, and it didn't have the rhythm of his. I heard a voice, and it was feminine. My curiosity was piqued. I stood, snagging a tissue off the desk and blowing my nose before hurrying down the hallway. I prayed I didn't look like I'd just been bawling my eyes out.

Susie stood outside with Cammi beside her. It was almost dark, and the automatic lights had come on. A second later, Daphne and Risa appeared. They were all here. My heart felt warm.

I waved through the glass, unlocking the door and opening it. "Hey."

"Hey, we were wondering about having a girls' night," Susie announced.

"Here?" I asked.

"Back at the gallery," Risa said. "Follow us over."

They walked with me through the

parking lot. Susie and Cammi had driven over together. Risa glanced my way, asking, "Can I ride back with you?"

"Sure."

"When we didn't see your car behind the gallery, we decided to come fetch you," she explained as she climbed into the passenger seat a few moments later.

I looked over at my landlord and friend and smiled. "I've been busy."

Risa simply nodded. The drive was only a few minutes. Just as we pulled into the parking lot, Risa said, "Fair warning, Susie is worried about you and Tucker. She's probably going to bring that up."

"Oh, god, what?"

"Apparently, Tucker told Daphne he's in love with you. Daphne told Flynn, and Cat overheard. Cat told Susie when she saw her at the coffee shop this morning. He said he's trying to give you space."

My mouth dropped. "Is this the telephone game?"

Risa's lips twitched with a smile. "It's a small town. We all want what's best for you. If that's Tucker, then we want him for you, but don't stress."

"People are gossiping about me, Risa. Nobody gossips about me. I'm nobody."

Her eyes narrowed, and she turned in the seat to face me as she unbuckled her seat belt. She reached for my hands, and I angled to face her. Our hands rested atop the console between the seats.

She studied me, her gaze intent. "You are *not* nobody. Nobody is nobody."

"Risa—" I began, but she cut me off.

"Listen to me, Skylar. I don't know your life story, and frankly, it's none of my business. We all have a past. I want to be your friend. I like you. I know you're kind of shy, and I get it because we all have that side. Some of us hide it better than others. No matter what happened in your life, you are someone, and you matter. Don't you ever, *ever* forget that."

Tears stung my eyes as I stared at her and nodded.

"Maybe that was kind of blunt, but we don't let our friends say they're nobody. It's totally against the rules."

"Okay," I whispered. "Thank you. I'm good at following the rules once I know them," I added dryly, my voice a little stronger.

"We all have to remind ourselves to shut that shitty voice up. That shitty voice is pretty loud sometimes. We all have that asshole in our brain on bad days or weeks or years. Tell her, or him, or whoever, to shut the fuck up. Now, let's go."

We climbed out of the car. Just before she opened the door to the gallery, I looked up at her. "Thank you."

"Anytime."

A few minutes later, Susie was doling out paper plates and slices of pizza, informing me that we'd only gotten pepperoni.

"Because everybody here likes pepperoni," Cammi offered.

Susie took a total of two bites before she brushed her curls off her shoulders. "What's going on with you and Tucker?"

I took a breath. "Susie, I don't know, and I have a small problem."

"Let us fix it," she said firmly.

"I don't know if you can fix it." I let out a startled laugh.

"We can try. Susie likes to fix everything," Cammi said dryly.

"I have a lot of baggage about relationships, and I tend to fall in love with everyone. My old therapist told me I was in love with the thought of being in love. I'm not sure if I'm in love with Tucker, but I'm in love with being in love with Tucker, and I feel crazy. He was distant for a few days, so I decided I needed to stop being stupid. Because I can't take it."

"Can't take what?" Daphne pressed.

"Getting desperate and feeling like I'm falling apart because some man doesn't love me," I said flatly.

"Oh." Susie eyed me, her gaze understanding. "But what if Tucker does love you? Maybe you should have a conversation with him."

"I probably should. I'm working up to it."

"Like I said before, I have a feeling about you and Tucker," Daphne offered softly.

I looked over at her, smiling. "I know, but—"

"Tucker loves you," she said solemnly. "You have to trust me on this."

I burst into tears. Then I discovered what it was like to have women who were actually nice and trying to be my friends fuss over me. It wasn't how I felt with Emily, that friend who knew me in a way no other friend could because of what we'd been through together. But it wasn't supposed to be how it was with her. My life was different now, and I was changing and growing. It was good in a different way.

I felt better, and I was able to laugh a little while later. I even scrambled up the nerve to ask Susie about Ludie's plans for the business and what to do when the timing was right.

"I am all over it," she said with an enthusiastic nod. "I helped Cammi get her business loan. We'll do it together. If anything legal needs to happen, Garrett is our guy."

"I met him," I replied. "He kind of intimidates me."

Risa laughed softly. "Yeah, he can come off that way, but I promise he's nice."

"I don't think I can afford to pay an attorney or you," I said honestly, glancing back at Susie.

Susie waved her hand airily. "I will help you for free because you're my friend. If it was a lot of work, I would be honest with you and tell you that I couldn't do it because I value my time. I already have all the forms lined out. We just fill in your info."

"You should specialize in doing something for women's businesses," Daphne said from her other side.

Susie glanced over, her eyes widening. "I should."

"You should," Daphne returned with a warm smile.

"Don't stress. We'll figure it all out," Susie

said with more confidence than I could muster.

After the group filtered apart, I went upstairs to my apartment, feeling a little bit better. I was going to be okay, no matter what happened with Tucker. Of course, I still missed him that night.

Staring at his last text the following morning, I finally mustered the nerve to reply.

Sure. Maybe we can see each other soon. Let me know when.

I thought I might avoid him a little while more just to get my bearings and somehow get rid of that panicky feeling in my heart whenever I thought about him, but Ludie got ahold of me.

"What is wrong with you?" she asked, hands on her hips as she eyed me one day at work.

"Nothing."

I suddenly worried I'd screwed up at work. "Did I mess up the ledger yesterday?"

"No! I'm talking about Tucker," she replied, her eyes narrowing with annoyance.

"Wh-what do you mean?" I sputtered.

"I screwed up a lot when I was younger, but I got something right. I married the right man for me. I'm not saying you have to marry

Tucker, but he *is* the right guy. He is a good man, and he loves you. You're afraid, so deal with it."

"Ludie!" I exclaimed, startled at her blunt assessment.

Dan's chuckle came over my shoulder, and I glanced back to see him in the hallway. "She has opinions, and she's usually right."

"Oh, my god," I muttered, my cheeks burning up.

"Don't be stupid. At least have the nerve to break up with him to his face," she added.

"I didn't—" I began.

She narrowed her eyes. "Don't lie to me. I ran into him. He said he tried to stop by and talk to you, but you had locked the place up. That's called being a coward." On the heels of a hard eye roll, she turned and walked out. "Girl, you're gonna lose a good man."

Chapter Thirty-Seven

SKYLAR

I spent most of that day trying not to be distracted. I managed, but barely. I thought I could do the easy thing and just cut my feelings out, slice them away, but it wasn't that easy. At all.

I kept missing Tucker, yet my doubts remained restless.

There were lots of things I didn't understand about other people, but I had a pretty good radar for when something was off. When you were in foster care, that sense became highly attuned. My therapist had once explained to me that it was a survival instinct. "You had to pay close attention because you didn't know what was going to happen."

Every time I thought about Tucker, which was a whole lot, my heart ached a little. It felt raw, like a painful scrape stinging.

I was startled to discover a phone message from my old social worker at the end of my workday. I made a habit of turning my phone off when I was at work. Ludie thought it was funny, but it was easy for me. Unlike most people my age, I hadn't had my own cell phone until I was an adult. Emily and I had shared one when we lived together for those years after we aged out of foster care. It was all we could afford. We never had our own phone like the other kids in high school. That was out of the question.

After Dan and Ludie left for the day, I resisted the urge to lock the doors, telling myself if Tucker stopped by that I would be brave and actually speak to him. I didn't want to admit that I was desperate for him to stop by while simultaneously praying he wouldn't.

Both options were terrifying.

I played Jolene's message. "Hi, Skylar. It's Jolene. I hope life is treating you well in Alaska. When you have a few minutes, please give me a call. I'm covering the on-call service tonight. I have something important for you."

"What the hell?" I muttered to myself.

Without hesitation, I tapped out the call number, laughing because I still had it memorized. It was the main call number for after-hours for the non emergency stuff for kids in foster care. There was also an emergency number, which was only for if you were on fire, or bleeding, or dying.

As promised, she picked up right away. "Skylar!" she exclaimed when she answered.

"Hey, Jolene."

It was odd to hear her voice. Emotion throttled in my throat at the sound of it. Although she was a professional and simply doing her job, I'd always felt kind of lucky that she'd been my social worker. So had Emily. She'd always checked in with us and made sure we stayed in the same school district for years. She did what she could for us under some shitty circumstances.

"How are you?" she asked, her tone warm.

"I'm okay," I answered.

"Yeah?" Her voice was soft, and I knew she was wondering if I missed Emily.

"I really am," I said, meaning it.

"Glad to hear it. I hope it's okay that I called."

"Of course, it is. What's up?"

She paused, and I could hear her take a breath. "I have a letter for you from Emily."

My lungs seized for a moment. "What?"

"I just got it, or I would have sent it sooner. When Emily was in the hospital before she died, she wrote a couple of letters. She gave them to the social worker at the hospital. I'm not sure why, but it took this long for it to get to me. That social worker didn't know how to find you. Emily was listed as your main contact for everything. She finally found me, and I told her I would be able to contact you."

Trepidation, anticipation, and grief rolled through me, one wave after another.

"Should I mail it to you?" she asked when I didn't say anything else.

"I'd like that, but could you email it too?" I didn't think I could wait for snail mail.

"Of course. I already have it scanned and sitting in a draft. I figured you'd want both. I'm sure you miss her."

I couldn't even speak. The next wave of grief slammed into me so hard I felt knocked over, gasping for air and trying not to swallow water. When I surfaced emotionally, I gulped in air while Jolene waited on the phone with me. I sensed she knew I was trying not to fall apart.

"I know she was family to you."

"She was," I whispered, my voice cracking and tears rolling down my cheeks.

"I know. You know you can call me any-time you need to talk."

I took a shaky breath. "I know, but I'm not your job anymore." That was the bald truth of our relationship.

She fell quiet for several beats before re-plying, "I know, but I actually care about you. If you ever need something, you know I can point you in the right direction. I'm really good at that." For a second, I thought I heard tears in her voice. "I met you because of my job, and you were my job. But, this, right here, I'm still here. I have boundaries. It's not like I'm doing anything crazy. I would tell my boss. 'Hey, I told Skylar she could call me if she needed something.' And she would say, 'Yeah, I get it. The world is hard, and foster kids don't have many people on their side.' Trust me, I know it's not easy."

"I know you do," I managed, swallowing through the tears wicking up from the knot in my throat.

"Will you send me a postcard?"

"Huh?"

"From Alaska. I've never been, but I've heard it's amazing. Is it as beautiful as they say?"

I smiled through my tears, smearing my free hand across my cheeks. "It really is. I'll mail you a postcard." I took a shaky breath.

"That'd be great. I already emailed the letter," she said just as my phone vibrated.

"Oh, I thought that was a text."

She laughed. "If you need anything, just call me, okay? I mean it."

"I will." I sniffled and took another breath. The air was amazing sometimes.

"Should we get off the phone now? You never were very good at saying goodbye and used to hang up on me a lot," she teased lightly.

I laughed because I *did* hang up on her a lot when I was a teenager. "Oh, my god. I was such a shitty kid to you sometimes."

"Now, cut that out. You were just like any other teenager, and you kept me on my toes," she said warmly.

"I won't hang up on you now."

"All right. You take care. My mailing address is on the signature in that email."

"It's okay for me to send a postcard?" I pressed.

Her sigh filtered through the line. "This job is complicated. You were on my caseload for ten years, and it matters to me how you're doing. If you want to send me postcards, I'd love your updates."

"Okay." My lips tugged into a smile.

"Let me confirm your mailing address before you go."

She recited it quickly. Of course, she had it right.

"How did you find that?"

"When people need something, we can look people up. I didn't have to do anything sketchy to find you."

I laughed, sniffling a little.

"You take care, Skylar. I'm going to put this letter in the mail tomorrow so you have the real copy."

"I really appreciate it. Thanks for calling me, Jolene. It's good to talk to you."

"Don't be a stranger," she returned.

Just as I was about to say goodbye, I said, "Hey, Jolene?"

"Yeah?"

"Thanks for everything. I always felt lucky that you were my social worker."

"You did?" She sounded surprised.

"Yeah. Not everybody gave a shit. You did."

"Well, thank you."

"And I promise I'll send you a postcard."

"I'm counting on it. Take care, Skylar."

"You too. Bye." I hung up quickly.

After we ended the call, I blew my nose and stared at my phone, where it sat innocuously on the desk. I had powered down the computers. It was just me sitting alone in the quiet office, afraid to read an email.

Yet I knew I couldn't wait. I snatched my phone up, tapping my email open. My eyes landed on the email from Jolene.

I gulped in a giant breath, squeezing my eyes shut before opening them wide.

Hi, Skylar. As promised, here's the letter. It'll go in the mail tomorrow now that I've confirmed your address. I wrote this before our call because I hoped you'd answer.

I'm really proud of you. You have a good job, and I'm glad you're somewhere you always wanted to go. Whether we talk again or not, I hope life treats you well from this point forward.

Fly for Emily.

All the best,
Jolene

Oh, wow. Tears were already rolling down my cheeks again. I dragged a tissue across my face and opened the attached letter she'd scanned in. My breath seized in my lungs when I saw Emily's familiar handwriting.

Dear Skylar,

They told me yesterday that I'm probably not going to survive. I've gotten some kind of infection that's all through my body, and I feel like shit. I'm okay, but I'm going to miss you like crazy. If there is a heaven, I'll be watching over you. I promise. Think of me as your guardian angel.

I'm asking you to make me one more promise. Try to make friends. You and I know nobody can make life okay for you except you. I know you've had shit luck with men. We both have. But if somebody good comes along, give him a chance. The assholes can fuck off.

I'm hoping you'll catch a lucky break. No matter what, take care of yourself. Put you first.

I hope you go to Alaska like we planned. We already signed the lease, and I sent you an email with all the information. Don't forget to open it.

High five with love,
Emily

. . .

Oh, hell. I was crying so hard I could hardly breathe. I heard the thump of my phone hitting the floor when I dropped it. I couldn't even manage to lean over and pick it up. I curled my knees into my chest, wrapping my arms around them and letting my head fall. I cried and cried and cried all over again.

Grief sucked. It really did feel like drowning. Sometimes, I would swallow water, then I would get some air, and then I would somehow tread for a little bit before sinking under the surface all over again.

I didn't hear anyone come in, but abruptly, I sensed someone was there. I lifted my head, spinning around in my chair, startled to see Tucker standing in the doorway.

"What are you doing here?" I asked, sniffling.

"Are you okay?" His eyes skated over my face.

I sighed because there was no point in trying to finesse my way out of this. "Of course, I'm not."

He was at my side in a flash, kneeling beside my chair. "What happened?"

"My friend, the one who died. She wrote me a letter when she was in the hospital, and my old social worker finally got it and found me. Well, it wasn't her, it was the hospital social worker who had it, and it took her that long to find someone to find me." I felt silly explaining it all.

"I'm sorry," he said.

Then Tucker wrapped me in his arms, and I tucked my head against his neck. I breathed, and I cried a little bit more, but I didn't completely fall apart. Several minutes later, I mumbled into his chest, and he prompted, "What?"

"I said it seems like I fall apart in front of you a little too much."

His hand was sliding up and down my back in a comforting pass. "Stop worrying about that. Losing someone you care about hurts like hell."

I lifted my head and took a breath, finally risking a look into his eyes. His gaze was steady and concerned. "You okay?" he asked.

I nodded, reaching for another tissue to wipe my eyes and blow my nose.

His eyes studied me. "I need to tell you something."

I braced myself. "Look, if you want to tell me we should just be friends and keep our distance, I already made that call. Don't worry. You don't have to tell me anything."

He held a hand up. "Hey, that's not what I want to tell you."

I sighed. "Okay, fine." I gestured to the empty chair near me.

He leaned back on his haunches before straightening and wheeling it closer to sit down.

"Okay, just get it over with." I circled my hand in the air.

"I had a girlfriend in high school. We were in love, and she died when I was seventeen."

"Um... Oh, wow, I'm sorry." That felt inadequate, but I didn't know what else to offer.

"I got a little distant because her mother sent me a letter. Before she died, she wrote some letters for friends and family and asked an attorney to wait before they were sent. In my case, that was fifteen years."

"Oh, you're thirty-two?" I asked. Leave it to me to focus on that mundane detail.

His lips lifted at one corner in a wry smile as he nodded. "I am."

"I'm twenty-eight."

"Good to know."

"I'm sorry about your girlfriend."

"Yeah, I am too. She had Ewing's sarcoma, fucking cancer. By the time they found it, it had already spread. We wanted her to beat the odds, but she didn't."

He took a quick breath as if bracing himself. I wanted to hold him and make it all go away.

"I figured I'd never fall in love again. I didn't want to because life is fucking unfair. But apparently, I did."

"Huh?"

"I love you."

The sound of my heartbeat rolled through my body. "Me?" I sniffled, staring hard at Tucker.

Chapter Thirty-Eight

TUCKER

Skylar blinked at me before her eyes narrowed, and she shook her head. "No."

"No, what?"

"There's no way you love me." Her voice was raspy, and her eyes held a stoic glint.

"I think I know how I feel."

My heart twisted at the doubt that came so readily for her. She didn't believe anyone would be there for her. Life had certainly taught her otherwise, but I wanted to prove her wrong. Even more than I had before.

She shook her head again, swiping at her tears with her knuckles. "How do you know?"

"Because I know what it feels like to love someone. And I love you. *You*."

She pressed her lips in a line. "I don't believe you," she announced.

"You don't have to, but I love you. I know this. And I know you have plenty of reasons not to believe in love. While I believe in love, I have plenty of reasons not to want to give love a chance again, but it doesn't change that I love you."

"What does it mean?"

"What does what mean?"

"What does it mean that you love me?"

"It means that I miss you when I'm not with you. It means I think about you just about all the time when I'm not otherwise occupied. It means that I hope you're okay all the time. It means I want to be the person you turn to when you're having a good day or a bad day. It means I want you to be that person for me. It means I feel like I won something when you smile. It means I know life has banged you up a little bit. It bangs everybody up. I love you just the way you are, a little cynical." She twisted her lips to the side. "Okay, maybe a lot cynical. A little doubtful. So independent and so brave. So loyal. It means I want to do this with you. I want it to be more than what we've had."

"What have we had?" she whispered.

"The best sex of my life. I don't want to keep fighting off falling in love with you. Instead, I'd rather just relax into it and let it be what it is and know that we can face what life throws our way together. I'm ready to give it a chance. I figure I've got a little luck on my side."

"How can you say that? You fell in love with someone in high school, and she died," Skylar said so bluntly it should have hurt.

But it didn't. It was a bracing breath of fresh air, the facts of what happened when I was younger. "I know. I've already been unlucky, so I figure maybe I have less of a chance of that happening again. The same goes for you. I don't expect you to tell me the same thing. I hope maybe I can earn your trust."

Skylar was quiet for several beats of my heart. Her eyes searched mine before dipping down. She slowly unfurled her arms from around her waist and laced her fingers together. She took a quick, sharp breath, almost as if she were bracing herself before her eyes lifted to mine again.

She whispered, "I already trust you, Tucker."

"You do?" This surprised me. I didn't

think Skylar trusted anyone. Faith and trust weren't something she handed out easily.

"I do." She looked down again, and I saw her shoulders rise as she drew in a gulp of air. This time when they lifted to mine again, she looked so vulnerable it was all I could do not to kneel in front of her, pull her in my arms, and just tell her it would all be okay. I would somehow make it okay. I would bend the will of the universe to mine.

"I don't want to tell you this, but I think I love you," she finally said, her voice as clear as a bell. My heart felt like a pair of hands loudly punching the sky.

"I used to be in love with falling in love. I thought I was in love all the time. I just wanted someone, anyone to love me, and I didn't have the best judgment in relationships and who to trust. But with you, I tried not to be in love with being in love. I tried really hard not to be desperate, and I don't actually feel desperate. Which is why I think I'm probably really in love." She swallowed, blinking rapidly.

For a few seconds, that guarded, vulnerable look in her eyes—a look I knew so well —fell away as we stared at each other. She blinked and looked down again.

"Thank you."

"For what?"

When she looked over at me again, her expression was almost shy. "For telling me how you felt and for trusting me."

"Well, you kind of make it hard not to," she grumbled.

My lips twitched with a smile. "Really?"

"Yeah, you're nice, honest, and straight-forward. You have good friends. Everybody says you're a great guy. I don't even know what to think. I usually date assholes."

"How about you not worry about it?"

"I worry all the time. You better be ready for that. Because if you can't handle that, well, you might as well forget about it."

I smiled. "I can handle it."

I stood, taking the two steps between our chairs and lifting her into my arms as I sat back down.

"What are you doing?" she squeaked.

"Holding you."

"Oh."

She was stiff for a second before she soft-ened and relaxed. She rested her head against my shoulder, and we sat there quietly. After a few moments, she lifted her head, peering up at me.

"What is it?" I prompted.

"I didn't expect this."

"Yeah, me neither. Join the club."

Skylar smiled, the joy in her eyes sending my heart flying.

We were going to go back to her place, but she pointed out that tonight was staff dinner at the lodge.

"Are you sure you want to do that?" I asked.

"Well, they expect you," she explained.

I laughed softly. "They do."

So we had dinner there.

Afterward, we lounged around the table, and Daphne glanced over at us. "So everything's okay?"

Skylar looked up at me. "Everything's great."

"Tell me what happened," Daphne pressed.

I decided to keep it simple. "I fell in love with Skylar."

When I glanced down at Skylar, her cheeks were bright pink.

Daphne let out a whoop. Everyone laughed, and then I remembered something.

"Hey, has anyone noticed that cargo container in the hangar near the public restrooms?" I asked.

Flynn looked puzzled. Nora shook her

head. Diego nodded. "Oh, yeah. Saw that the other day."

I glanced down at Skylar. "Told you."

She burst out laughing. Then we finally went back to Skylar's place.

Chapter Thirty-Nine

SKYLAR

I felt stripped bare emotionally as if all my defenses had fallen away. As vulnerable as I felt, I meant what I'd said. I trusted Tucker completely. It felt serendipitous that we both got letters from people who meant something different to each of us that basically told us not to be stupid.

Tucker was kissing me, and we had just walked in. My back was pressed against the door. I was the one who started it. I'd yanked him down because I needed to kiss him. I needed the physical, visceral sensation.

He broke free. The sound of our ragged breathing filled the air. He stared down at me, saying, "We're going to your bedroom."

"The door's fine," I teased.

His chuckle was gruff as he lifted me in his arms and carried me across the living room and into my bedroom. He undressed me slowly. I felt as if I were a gift just for him.

His hands mapped my body. His touch was gentle and sensual and sent licks of fire over my skin everywhere he touched me with sparks flying into the air around us.

He murmured hot, sweet, and dirty words. By the time he spread me out on the bed, and his weight came down over me, I was melted, liquid, and so needy I was gasping and begging for him. I was not one to plead, but I had never felt as desperate as I did then. I always held something back, but this felt different.

The reckless edge that came with sex for me was gone. This was so intimate. I almost couldn't bear it. When I felt the nudge of him at my core followed by the thick glide as he filled me, I cried out. My orgasm startled me with its swiftness and ferocity. He held me tight, staying with me through it. He flew with me this time.

Afterward, he held me close and re-mained with me through the night. I felt the opposite of alone, so interconnected emotionally I couldn't sense where my feelings ended and his began.

EPILOGUE

Skylar

A year and a half later

Ludie stood behind me in the mirror with her head cocked to the side. She lifted a hand and smoothed it over the back of my hair. "You look lovely, and you know I'm not one for compliments."

I snorted at her honesty. She was helping me get ready for my wedding. Dan was walking me down the aisle. While I was wearing an actual wedding dress, which was still a little shocking to me, Ludie was wearing a practical pair of slacks with a blouse. She'd held her hand up when I saw her, announcing, "This is as dressy as I get."

My wedding dress was simple. It wasn't white, but I had a reason. I wanted to wear my favorite color, which I shared with Emily. It was a deep sapphire blue.

Daphne had taken it upon herself to help me find a wedding dress, clucking and shaking her head and telling me she didn't trust me to do it myself. When I asked why, she'd said, "Because you don't realize how beautiful you are, and you'll try to hide it."

The result was a silk sheath with a lovely curved neckline. The blue set off my dark hair. I'd eschewed a veil because I thought it would be annoying, which had amused Daphne.

Ludie turned me around. She rested her hands on my shoulders before lifting them to cup my cheeks. She surprised me when she leaned forward to press a quick kiss on my cheek.

In the year since Tucker had asked me to marry him, I'd learned many things about Ludie and Dan, including that they had a daughter who passed away from an accidental drug overdose. Of course, it had shattered their hearts.

Ludie had told me she felt like I was their second daughter. "The daughter of our heart," she'd said.

Every time I thought about that, I almost burst into tears.

"You did good," she said as she dropped her hands from my cheeks and rested them on her hips.

"Daphne picked out my dress."

"Well, thank God for her because you wouldn't have wanted me to dress you, but your dress isn't what I'm talking about. You did good with Tucker. He's a good man, and he is solid. When people are young, they don't know what to look for in a partner," she said with a cluck.

I knew perfectly well Tucker was the only decent guy I'd ever had a relationship with. Of course, maybe that wasn't fair to the guys I'd glommed onto like a barnacle in my younger years. I'd been young and stupid, and so had they. None of us knew what we wanted. Maybe some of them were still assholes, and maybe some of them turned out to be nice guys later on.

Tucker was a *really* good guy, and sometimes, I still couldn't believe he loved me. One of my favorite things about him was his tendency to be bluntly honest. When he gave me a compliment, I knew he meant it.

"I'm glad you think so. I trust you, so I

know you'd tell me if I'd fallen for the wrong
guy."

Ludie eyed me quietly for several beats
before nodding firmly. "My opinion does matter, but don't ever live your life based on the
opinions of others. Mine only matters because I love you. If you'd picked the wrong
guy, I'd have kicked his ass and chased him
out of your life."

I burst out laughing, which was better
than bursting into tears. I didn't want to ruin
the pretty violet eye shadow Daphne had
done. It was subtle, and it set my eyes off.

"Dan's waiting for you. He's wearing a
suit." Ludie leaned forward as if imparting a
deep secret.

I still saw Ludie and Dan almost every
day, although our roles had switched. They'd
handed control of the business over to me. I
hadn't ended up needing that bank loan because they'd refused to sell it, but I'd worked
with Garrett to ensure everything was handled properly on the legal end. While Ludie
and Dan worked a lot less, they still stopped
in almost daily to check on things. I loved
seeing them, not to mention having them
there to help steer me on the logistics helped
immensely with my anxiety at taking on a
business.

I smiled. "Thank you, Ludie. For everything."

For just a second, I thought maybe I saw the glimmer of tears in her eyes.

The rest of the afternoon passed in a blur. I remembered Dan's hand on my elbow as he walked me down the aisle. I remembered stopping at the front of the small group of friends and made family gathered for Tucker and me. There was a trellis with flowers and the ocean glittering under the sun behind us.

I barely remembered the ceremony, except for looking into Tucker's bright blue eyes, blue as the sky. I remembered him saying, "I do," and me repeating the words and managing not to cry. The threat of ruining my makeup was the only thing that held me back.

I remembered the reception better than the ceremony. With my new friends toasting me, I looked around and realized I'd done it. I'd come to Alaska all by myself. I'd learned that families were made, and I had made one for myself.

I saw my dream with Emily through to fruition. I still missed her, and I always would. But I kept my promise to her and, more importantly, to myself.

That night we were staying in my apartment, and the next day, Tucker was flying us in one of his planes to Fireweed Harbor, a tiny town in Southeast Alaska that was promised to be beautiful. We were staying in a private resort, and I couldn't wait. Tucker had suggested a tropical vacation, but I didn't want one. I loved Alaska. It was home.

That night, we stepped out on the small balcony at my apartment, and I leaned my arms on the railing. When I lifted my chin, the salty sea breeze gusting off the ocean whisked across my cheeks. I felt Tucker come up behind me, sliding his arms around my waist.

"Hey there," he murmured.

I angled my head up, glancing over my shoulder. "Hey." I smiled.

"How do you feel?" he asked.

"Pretty good. You?"

"That's it? Just pretty good?" he teased.

I turned in his arms. "Okay, amazing," I returned lightly. That was actually the truth.

He dipped his head, brushing his lips over mine. "Perfect because I'm better than amazing," he replied against my mouth. "You ready?" He straightened.

"For what?"

"Life. It's day one. We're officially a

team." I could see the twinkle in his eyes from the moonlight falling across us.

I pressed a palm to his chest, something I did often. It was a way to ground myself, to remind myself he was here, he was real, and he was mine. His heart thudded, strong and true, against my touch.

"Of course, I'm ready."

From the day I decided to stop running from my feelings for Tucker, our path hadn't been a straight line, not emotionally, that is. It was hard for me to have faith in something good. While that faith came easier to Tucker, I still saw those shadows chase through his eyes every so often. I knew that he knew what real loss was like, that letting yourself fall in love meant putting that on the line every single day.

I silently thanked his old high school girl-friend once in a while. I wished he hadn't had to lose her, but I was grateful for the letter she wrote when she knew she was dying. Without it, I didn't know if he ever would have taken the risk. I didn't know if I would have without the letter from Emily. It's funny how people could reach through time and give you a little nudge.

. . .

Want a glimpse of the future for Tucker & Skylar? Join my newsletter to receive an exclusive scene:

Sign   up   here: https:// BookHip.com/NJLCXAF

p.s. If you are already subscribed, you'll still be able to access the scene.

Coming soon is Keep Me Close in the Light My Fire Series. Hallie's looking for an escape. Just for one night. No last names, no phone numbers.

Chase gives her exactly what she needs, and they never expect to see each other again. Until Hallie discovers she's pregnant.

She only has one way to find the man who she thought would be nothing but a memory.

Don't miss Chase & Hallie's story - it's hot, emotional. Chase is just the protective hero you need!

Pre-order Keep Me Close - due out June 28, 2022!

For more swoony romance...

This Crazy Love kicks off the Swoon Series - small town southern romance with enough heat to melt you! Jackson & Shay's story is epic - swoon-worthy & intensely emotional. Jackson just happens to be Shay's brother's best friend. He's also *seriously* easy on the eyes. Shay has a past, the kind of past she would most definitely like to forget. Past or not, Jackson is about to rock her world. Don't miss their story! Free on all retailers!

Burn For Me is a second chance romance for the ages. Sexy firefighters? Check. Rugged men? Check. Wrapped up together? Check. Brave the fire in this hot, small-town romance. Amelia & Cade were high school sweethearts & then it all fell apart. When they cross paths again, it's epic - don't miss Cade's story!
Free on all retailers!

For more small town romance, take a visit to Last Frontier Lodge in Diamond Creek. A sexy, alpha SEAL meets his match with a brainy heroine in Take Me Home. Marley is all brains & Gage is all brawn. Sparks fly when their worlds collide. Don't miss Gage & Marley's story!
Free on all retailers!

If sports romance lights your spark, check out The Play. Liam is a British footballer who falls for Olivia, his doctor. A twist of forbidden heats up this swoon-worthy & laugh-out-loud romance. Don't miss Liam & Olivia's story.
Free on all retailers!

ACKNOWLEDGMENTS

Every book is a journey, and at the end come the readers. Huge thanks to every reader who takes a chance on my stories!

Much appreciation to my assistant who sweeps up the details I forget. To my editor for helping me polish Tucker & Skylar's story, and to Terri D. for patiently proofreading and making sure I don't mess up my days of the week and then some. And, to my early readers who catch the stubborn errors and kindly let me know.

Gracious thanks to the bloggers who share my books and those of so many others who cheer on the joy of romance.

My dogs nap through chapters and get me outside when my brain needs time to plot. To DBC for putting up with my schedule and tolerating hours of me disappearing into my office.

xoxo
J.H. Croix

ABOUT THE AUTHOR

USA Today Bestselling Author J.H. Croix lives in a small town in Maine with her husband and three spoiled dogs. Croix writes contemporary romance with sassy women and alpha men who aren't afraid to show some emotion. Her love for quirky small-towns and the characters that inhabit them shines through in her writing. Take a walk on the wild side of romance with her bestselling novels!

Places you can find me:
jhcroixauthor.com
jhcroix@jhcroix.com

 facebook.com/jhcroix
 instagram.com/jhcroix
 bookbub.com/authors/j-h-croix

www.ingramcontent.com/pod-product-compliance
Lightning Source LLC
Chambersburg PA
CBHW070748190726
48292CB00002B/456